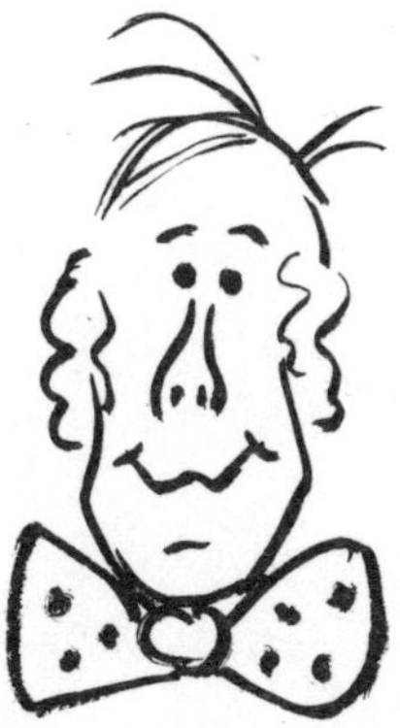

Author

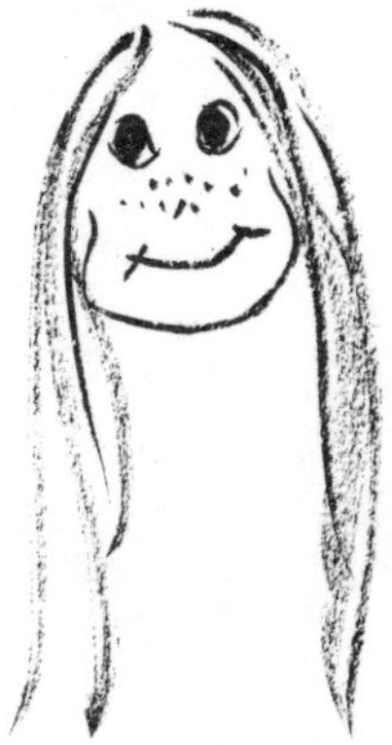

Artist

About This Book

Of the twenty-one books he has produced, Pierre Berton insists that this is his favourite, possibly because its five human characters bear a suspicious resemblance to his own children. First published in 1962, it has become a Canadian classic, bringing the author more enthusiastic fan mail than anything else he has written. No week goes by that does not bring at least a dozen letters and drawings from children giving their own pictorial versions of the Og story. One class in New York state recently sent him a hand carved plaque to mark his creation. On four different occasions, in classrooms as far apart as Toronto and Honolulu, the book has been turned into a play. Now that the original generation of Og enthusiasts is beginning to produce a new generation of Og readers, the book is being re-issued with fresh illustrations in colour and black-and-white. There are more than 150 of them, all the work of the author's daughter, Patsy, a student at the Camberwell School of Art in London, England. We think Patsy is the ideal person to illustrate *The Secret World of Og* because, as the story makes clear, she was there when it all happened.

Jeff,
Here's to little green monsters + our 1st novel.
☺ RP May 2001

The Secret World of OG

The Secret World

McClelland and Stewart

# of OG

by Pierre Berton
newly illustrated by
Patsy Berton
(who was there)

Reprinted 1975, 1977, 1978

0-7710-1386-8

The Canadian Publishers
McClelland and Stewart Limited
25 Hollinger Road, Toronto

Printed and bound in Canada

Dedicated to all Five...

**...and to
Peggy Anne
and Perri
who weren't
born when
it happened**

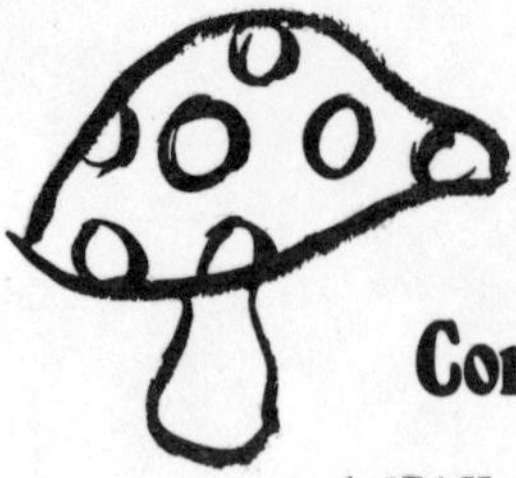

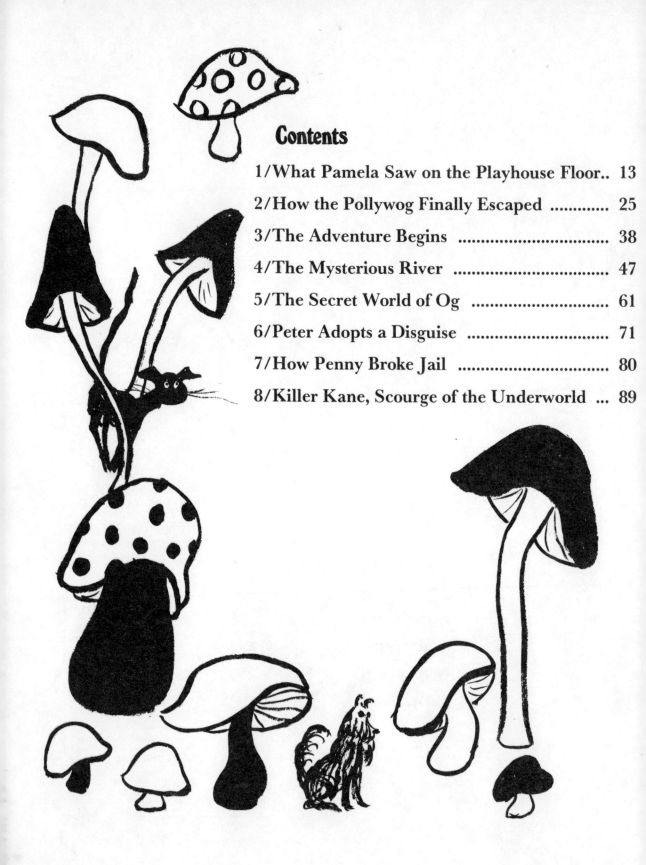

Contents

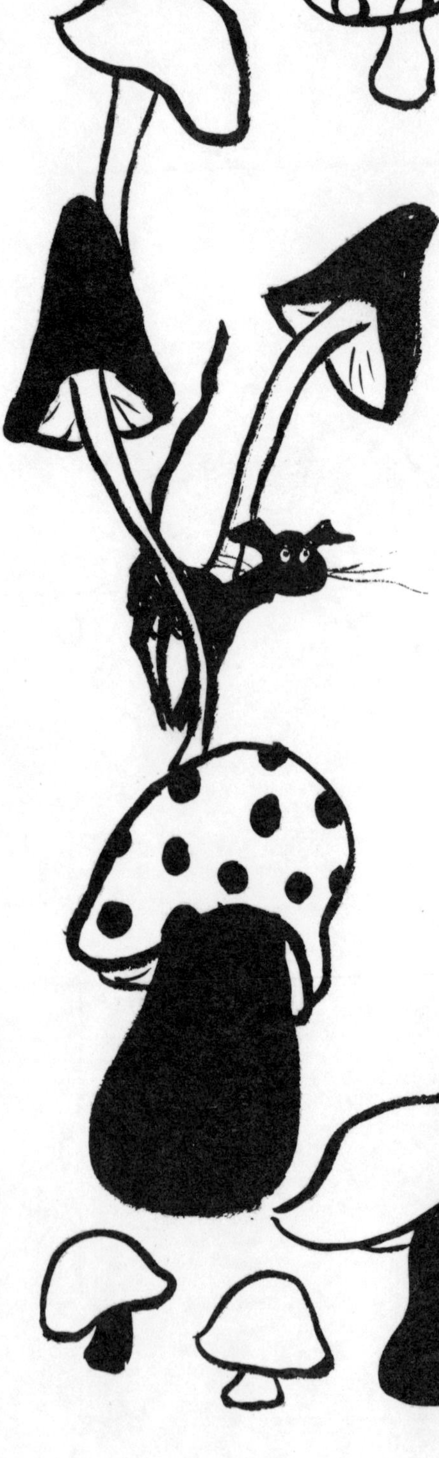

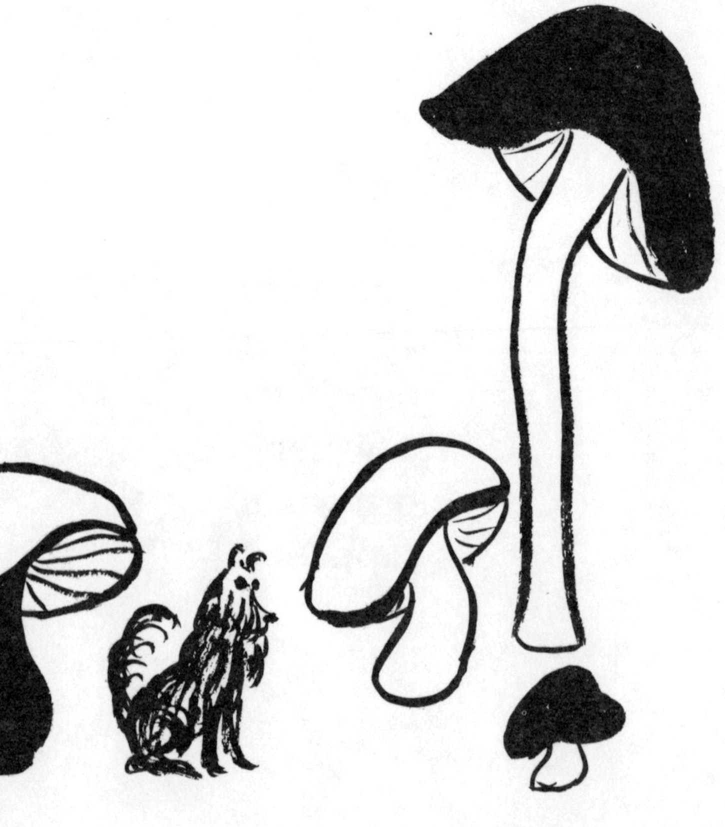

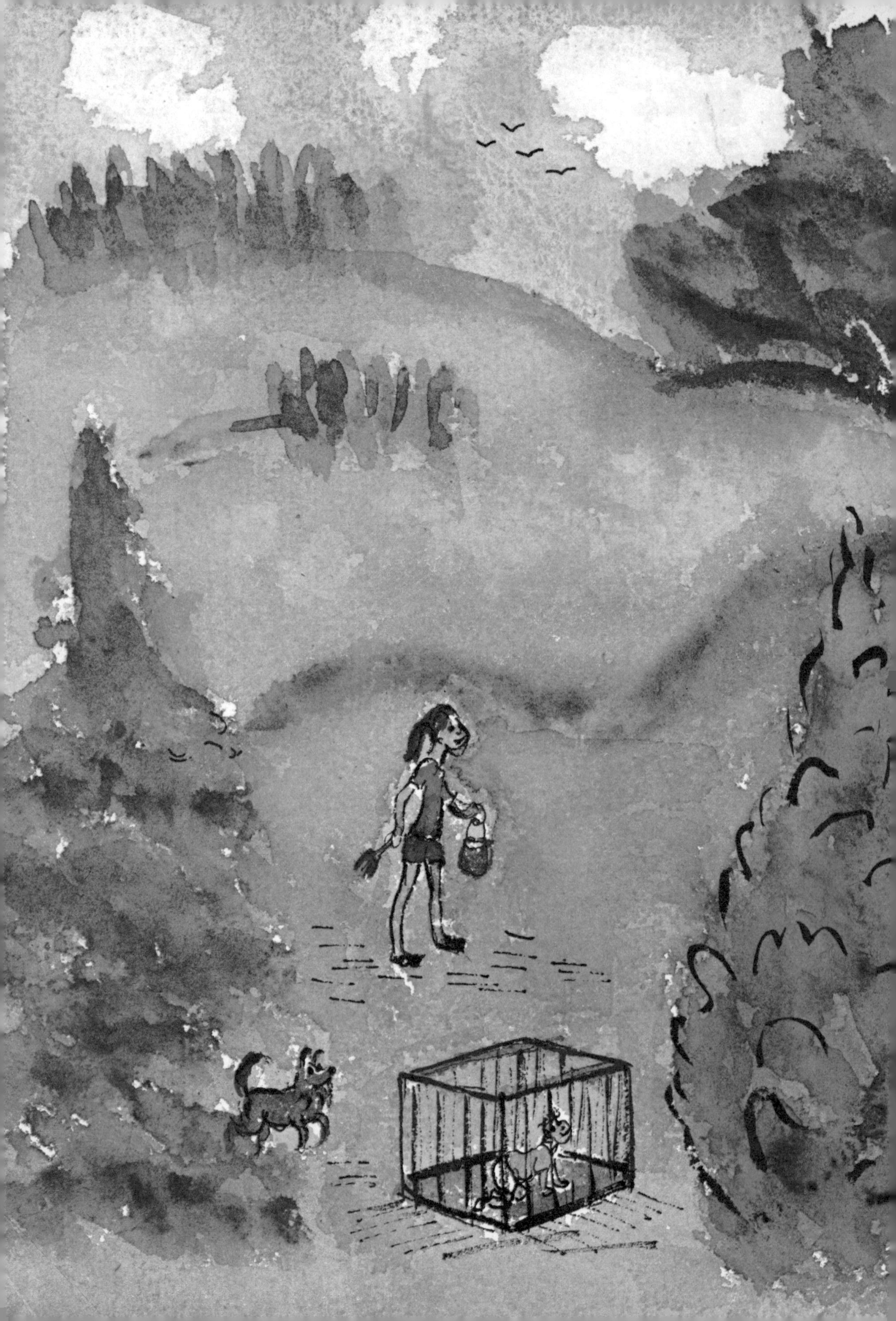

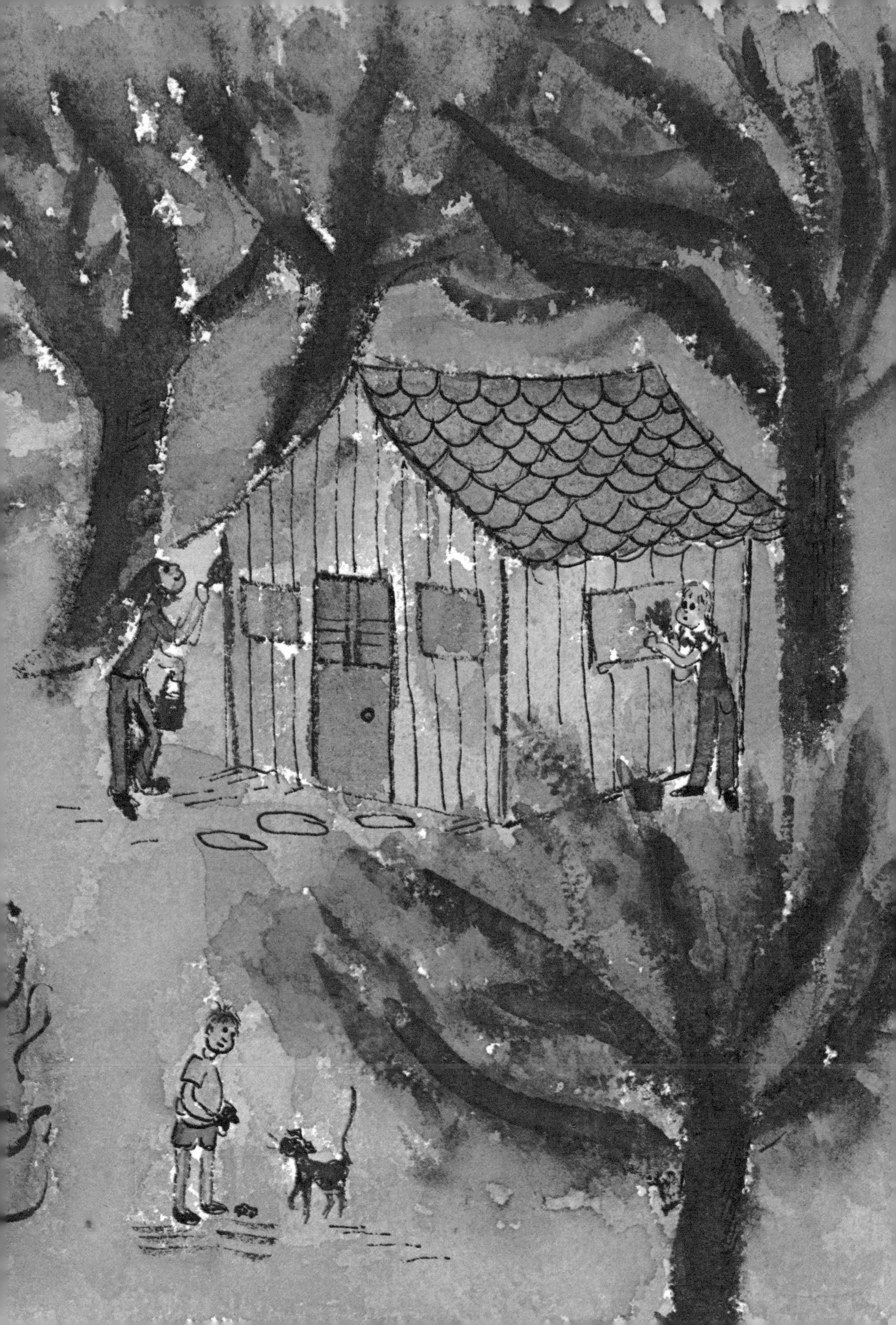

1/What Pamela Saw on the Playhouse Floor

There were five children, counting the Pollywog, and their names all began with the letter P. Why that should be no one was quite sure but Father said it was done purposely so that it would be easier to divide up the silverware when they all got married.

At any rate that's how it was. The eldest was Penny. (Her name was Penny and not Penelope because Father said he wouldn't have a daughter of his named Penelope.)

Next there was Pamela whom most people called plain Pam, all except Father who deliberately called her Pamela because he said no self-respecting daughter of his ought to be called Pam.

Then there was Patsy whose full name, which nobody ever used, was Patricia Dorothy, and Peter who was often called Pete, and finally Paul who was usually called Polly or The Pollywog and who was just one year old.

On the day that It happened (and the children always referred to what happened as "It") , Penny, Pamela and Patsy were re-painting the Playhouse. Peter was playing with his toy tractor. And the Pollywog, as usual, was in jail.

The Playhouse was situated several hundred yards from the house where the children lived and ate and slept,

and that is why "It" was able to happen at all. The children lived in the open countryside, and the Playhouse, which looked like a real house, had been built underneath a group of large elm trees.

The House had a door that really locked and windows that really opened. There were pink curtains on the windows and bright blue linoleum on the floor. There was a little cot and a Treasure Chest and a pretend phone and several small cupboards. In the cupboards were tiny boxes which looked like real boxes with real names of soap and flour and cake mixes and other things on them. Inside the boxes were small brightly coloured candies.

The Playhouse belonged to Penny because she was the oldest. She was very serious about it. She had a small broom and a small mop and a small pail and a toy carpet sweeper and every single day she cleaned that Playhouse until it shone. Quite often Pamela helped her because, by helping, Pamela felt that she owned a piece of the Playhouse. There were arguments about this but it was generally agreed that Pamela owned more of it than Patsy, who helped only occasionally.

Patsy was very energetic when she helped, but being younger than the other two she was apt to cause trouble. She would slosh water all over the cot and try to scrub the sheets with the wet mop. On this particular day when Penny and Pamela were re-painting the outside of the Playhouse, Patsy, who was helping, painted both windows.

This caused a great deal of trouble, when it was discovered.

Penny, who had been painting vigorously and very neatly, being careful to get the edges right, stepped back to look over the job.

"The windows have gone!" she said suddenly, and with just a trace of panic.

"Windows can't go," said Pamela, calmly. Pamela kept on painting, rather slowly, for she did not believe that overwork was very good for people.

"But I tell you they've *gone*, Pam!" Penny shouted. "They've just simply vanished!" And she began to run around the Playhouse, looking for the windows.

"Maybe Patsy painted over them," said Pamela, still painting slowly but steadily.

Patsy, who at that moment had just finished painting both her shoes a lovely green, looked up and then stood up and began to back away. As she did so she stuffed a tube of green paint mix in her pocket. You never know when that sort of thing might come in handy.

Penny stopped and turned on her sister.

"Patsy! *You didn't!*" she screamed.

Patsy had been about to invent an imaginative story that a goblin had done it when nobody was looking. Then she saw Penny's face and decided not to.

"Nobody told me," she said, still backing away.

"That's right," said Pamela, who was still painting away, slowly but steadily. "Nobody *did* tell her."

"She should have known!" shouted Penny. She would have liked to smack Patsy a good one, but she wasn't sure it would be worth it. Patsy had a scream like a noon-day whistle and Penny could see that she was prepared to use it. Then Mother would come and everybody would talk at once and Mother would end up making them all do chores.

"If we hurried with the cloth we could clean all the paint off the windows," said Pamela. "It's still wet."

She said this as if it were an interesting news item, but made no effort to get a cloth. Instead she kept on painting.

"Well, hurry then!" cried Penny, rushing into the Playhouse and getting two big cloths and shoving one into Pamela's hands. "Don't just sit there! No, not you, Patsy,

you're not allowed to help any more! Go on off and play with the twins. You're not allowed in the Playhouse until I say so!"

"O-*kay!*" said Patsy defiantly, digging her hands into the pockets of her blue jeans where two frogs, a toad and a pet garter snake named Snavely greeted them with instant curiosity. Patsy decided she might use her tube of paint to re-colour the frogs green; she had noticed lately that they were getting rather faded.

"It was all too jalopy for me, anyway," said Patsy to herself but loudly enough for Penny to hear.

"What's she mean by '*jalopy*'?" Penny asked Pamela as they began to wipe the paint clean from the windows.

"It's just a word she and the twins invented," said Pamela. "It's part of their secret language. Half the time I can't understand a word they say."

Patsy, by this time, was trudging across the field in the bright afternoon sunlight, heading for the home of the Terrible Twins, who lived down the road. The twins were her closest friends and allies, being exactly the same age. Like Patsy they had angelic faces and blonde heads. Like Patsy, they liked frogs better than people and snakes better than frogs. The three of them had once captured a skunk and put him in a paper shopping bag and taken him home. They said they did this to surprise Mother, and of course it had surprised her quite a bit.

The two older girls quickly got the paint off the windows.

"I'm tired of painting," Pamela said. "Let's go in the Playhouse and read."

"We ought to finish first," said Penny.

"Oh, Penny, it's too hot! Come *on!*"

"Well . . ." said Penny dubiously. She really didn't

want to paint any more that day but she disliked starting something and not finishing it.

"Just for an hour," said Penny, and the two dropped their brushes and went inside. Pamela lay down on the Treasure Chest (which was full of Dress-Up clothes) and plunged into her latest *Mad Monster* comic book. Penny lay down on the cot and turned to Page 32 of *Lucy Lawless, Girl Pirate,* which was book No. 27 in the Lucy Lawless series.

Pamela had scarcely started the *Mad Monster* comic book before she began to giggle and hug herself with glee. As the magazine was clearly labelled "comic," Pamela knew that it must be funny. She thought the Mad Monster was the funniest thing she had ever seen, except for Black Bart of Tombstone, the television cowboy. As a matter of fact, Pamela thought most things were funny – even when they weren't supposed to be. When Black Bart mounted his faithful horse Quicksand and shouted to his faithful Indian friend, Grunto, Pamela laughed so hard she often rolled right off her chair.

"Oh, stop giggling, Pam," said Penny. "I can hardly read when you giggle like that."

"I can't help it," Pamela said. "The Mad Monster has just eaten fifteen people alive and now he's gone off to his secret lair on the planet Mars."

"I don't see what's so funny about *that,*" Penny said.

"It's almost as funny as Black Bart," Pamela said, and turned the page to see how Garth Greatheart would manage to capture the Mad Monster, as he always did at the end of each story. Garth Greatheart had enormous muscles, like Popeye, and wore an extremely odd blue and red suit with a flowing cape. Pamela began to giggle as soon as she saw his picture.

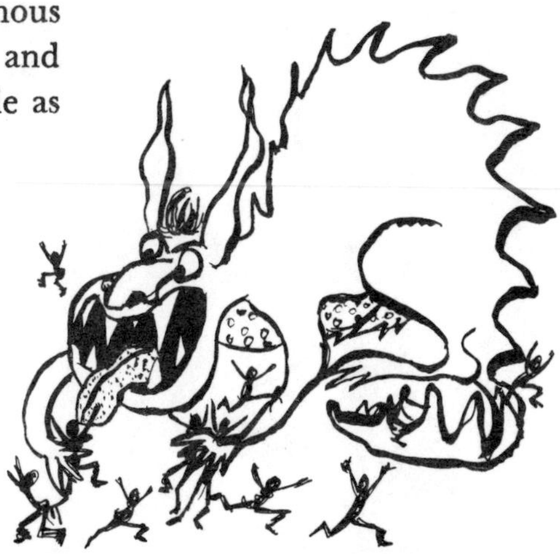

"Garth Greatheart is a boob," said Pamela to herself and began to giggle all over again.

"Pamela!" said Penny, standing up and putting her book down. "If you make any more noise you're going to have to leave the Playhouse."

"I'll stay quiet," said Pamela amiably, and instead of laughing out loud she continued to laugh, but quietly to herself. She had practised this ever since she was a small baby in her crib. In those days she had thought everything was funny but so many people poked at her that she stopped laughing out loud. Instead she put on a solemn expression and laughed inside.

"What a solemn, serious little girl!" people used to say, looking at Pamela with her big round brown eyes and her blank expression. Pamela didn't mind them saying that. She thought it was a huge joke and giggled to herself – but inside.

Penny was lost in Lucy Lawless. Her favourite books were those about Romance and Adventure – the more dramatic the better. Before she learned to read she had been fed a steady diet of books about Good Little Children, who Helped Mummy in the Kitchen. They had pretty pictures but no real story. As Penny often said, she liked a book that had a real story to it. At school, when she was learning to read, the books seemed to have no story at all. They had all been about very dull children who talked in monosyllables saying "Look! Look!" and "Oh! Oh!" over and over again. These children never seemed to get into any trouble. As Penny remarked when she was six, "They never meet giants or ogres or get killed or anything like that. All they do is go to the store with their Mummy."

Pamela thought the school books were hilarious and had sometimes disturbed the quiet of the schoolroom by laughing out loud in the middle of a Reading lesson. But

Penny, once she learned to read, had sworn she'd never read another dull book in her life.

There were forty-five books in the Lucy Lawless series and Penny had read twenty-seven of them. She kept a small notebook with the titles carefully noted down, and the numbers, so that she wouldn't read one twice by mistake. There was *Lucy Lawless, Girl Welder*; *Lucy Lawless, Girl Skin Diver*; *Lucy Lawless, Girl Card Sharp*; *Lucy Lawless, Girl Taxidermist* and many others. Lucy Lawless was a sort of modern-day Robin Hood and although she was sometimes engaged in shady practices the author made it clear that she stole from the rich only to give to the poor. Penny however had a sneaking suspicion that Lucy Lawless kept *some* of the money for herself.

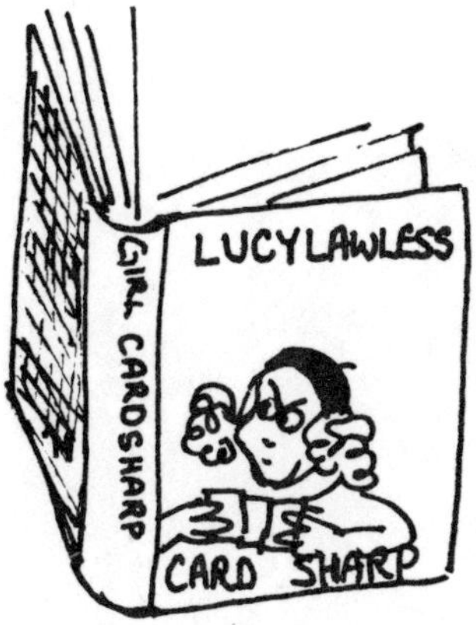
LUCYLAWLESS
GIRL CARDSHARP
CARD SHARP

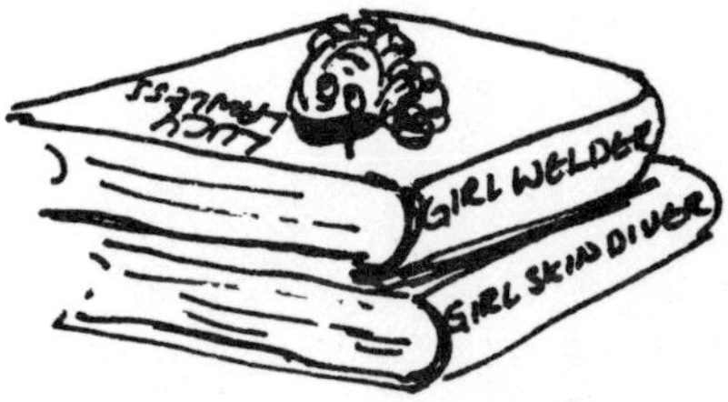
GIRL WELDER
GIRL SKIN DIVER

Penny had even written a letter in her large round hand, to the local television station, urging that Lucy Lawless be made into a television series. She had a feeling that it would be even better than *I Was a Teen Age Private Eye* which was her favourite at the moment. Maybe, she thought, they could even get Alfred La Verne, the fourteen-year-old singing sensation, to play in it. This combination of the world's greatest author and the world's greatest singer sent a delicious little thrill down Penny's spine. Sometimes in her day dreams she saw herself being led onto an enormous stage to meet Lucy Lawless and Alfred La Verne in person.

"And here is the little lady who started it all," the master of ceremonies would say. "Without her inspiration, the famous Lucy Lawless series would never have been made possible."

And then she would shake hands with Alfred La Verne and ask him to come out and visit the Playhouse and they would all have tea together, yes, Pam, too – and even Patsy, Penny thought generously.

If only Elizabeth Anne could be there to share in the joy of it all, she thought sadly, but Elizabeth Anne was gone, probably forever. She had been Penny's very favourite doll, given to her three Christmases before, and she loved her like her own child. She had golden hair that really combed and legs that really walked. Then, three weeks before, Penny had left Elizabeth Anne outside the Playhouse by mistake overnight. The next morning she had rushed out to get her but Elizabeth Anne was gone. No amount of searching produced her and Penny had never quite gotten over the loss.

As Penny lay lost in Lucy Lawless, Pamela came to the end of her Mad Monster book. With a motion born of habit, she reached almost automatically for another from the stack piled on the floor.

As she did so she happened to look about the Playhouse and it was then that she saw a strange thing. It was so strange, indeed, that Pamela did not open the new comic book, but just watched, in fascination.

A tiny little saw, quite the smallest and thinnest (and sharpest) saw that Pamela had ever seen, was protruding from the floorboards of the Playhouse. It was sawing away diligently, propelled by an unseen hand. It came up right through the linoleum, working its way across the floor. Then it turned in a new direction and sawed away some more. Pamela realized that somebody or something, beneath the Playhouse, was engaged in sawing out a square of the floor.

Pamela watched the sharp little saw in silence. It did not occur to her to mention it to Penny, who was devouring Lucy Lawless. If Pamela told people even half of what she saw, she would be talking all the time and it was not her nature to talk all the time. Moreover if she told one quarter of what she saw, people would not believe her. She knew this because she had tried.

For Pamela saw a great deal that others did not see. At

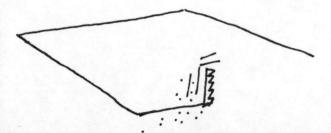

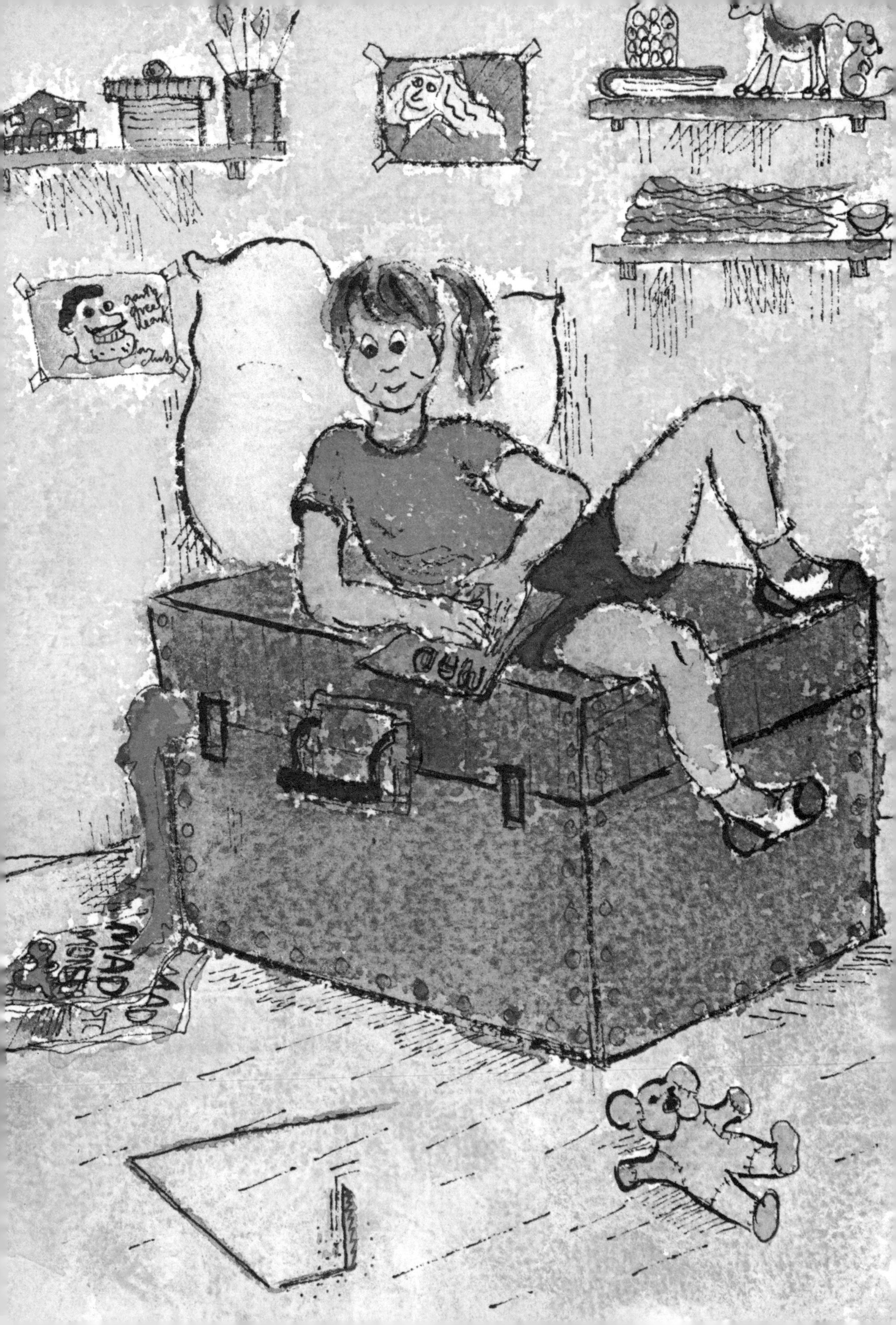
MAD

school she would often look up from her books, which she thought dull, and see odd things in the school yard.

Once, in the middle of her Number Facts, she had looked up and seen two very small fairies with gossamer wings, seated on the window sill. The fairies were gossiping together, Pamela decided. She wished she could understand what they were saying but they were so small she could not hear.

Her teacher asked her a question three times and Pamela did not hear, so interested was she in the little fairies.

The teacher walked down the aisle and talked into Pamela's ear and still Pamela did not hear. The teacher then rapped Pamela across the knuckles with a blackboard eraser and Pamela slowly turned about and saw her.

"I'm sorry," Pamela said. "I was just watching two little fairies gossiping."

And her eyes were so big and her expression so solemn that the teacher did not actually disbelieve her. She simply told Pamela to attend to her Number Facts. She had long since learned that you could not push Pamela into anything.

The odd thing was that, though she spent half her time in a small private world of her own, Pamela did quite well at her lessons.

Once during a Social Studies examination she had looked out of the window and seen an old man in the sky looking down at her. The old man had a long white beard and his face was inexpressibly sad. He was the saddest man Pamela had ever seen and she fell to wondering who he was and why he was sad and whether, up in the sky, he was allowed to drink chocolate milk and other things like that.

Her teacher glanced up and saw Pamela staring

solemnly out of the window while the other children scribbled furiously on their ruled paper.

"It will teach her a lesson," thought the teacher, and decided not to interrupt.

The only thing was that, when the papers were marked, Pamela was found to have 80 per cent.

Indeed she did almost as well in her classes as Penny, who studied with great energy and led her class. Penny always got good remarks on her report card. The fact was that she studied so hard her teachers were afraid she would become sick from overwork.

"Penny is an exceptionally good student," the remarks on her June report card had read. And the remarks on Pamela's report card read: "Pamela *could* be an exceptionally good student if only she would apply herself." That was teacher-talk meaning Pamela looked out the window too much. The strange thing was, however, that both girls had got very similar marks.

When she was smaller Pamela had chattered cheerfully about the things she saw as she looked about her. Now she said less. She used to tell her mother about the elves she had seen eating the high-bush cranberries and of the troll she had observed taking a shower in the bathroom when no one was looking. Nobody took her seriously.

So this is why Pamela now said nothing at all as the tiny little saw slowly cut a square in the centre of the Playhouse floor.

Whoever was sawing away was very neat about it, Pamela decided. She wondered if the end of the square, when it was cut, would join up with the beginning of the square. It did – exactly. Pamela waited to see what would happen next.

Very slowly the square piece in the middle of the floor

began to lift, at one end. Soon a hand appeared underneath it and then an arm. The hand was very small and delicate and the arm very thin. They must belong to somebody awfully strange, Pamela thought, because they were quite green in colour.

A moment later a small head appeared. It, too, was quite green and the eyes were even bigger than Pamela's. Pamela looked straight into the eyes, without changing expression. The eyes blinked, the head vanished, and the square piece of the floor snapped back into place hurriedly.

She waited for a moment to see if the little green face would appear again but nothing happened. Outside in the distance she could hear the squeals of Patsy and the twins, on the hunt for snakes and toads. Behind the Playhouse several chipping sparrows and a cedar waxwing chattered pleasantly in the trees. The afternoon sun poured in through the Playhouse window leaving a bright square piece of light almost on the spot where the little saw had done its work. On the cot, opposite, Penny came to Chapter Eight of *Lucy Lawless, Girl Pirate*.

Pamela completed the motion which had been arrested a few moments before. She pulled another comic book from the tattered pile beside her and noticed, with satisfaction, that it was a recent edition of *Larry the Ghoul*.

By the time she reached the first knifing scene she was laughing uncontrollably to herself. Sometimes, she thought, Larry the Ghoul was almost as funny as Black Bart, the Scourge of Tombstone.

2/How the Pollywog Finally Escaped

Although the others tried to shoulder some of the blame for what happened that afternoon, Penny always blamed herself. She should have known better than to turn her back on the Pollywog, even for five minutes, she said.

"Well," Pamela would always say when they discussed it later, " if you *hadn't*, It never would have happened."

"I know," Penny would answer, "but that doesn't excuse it. Suppose they'd eaten him or something? Then how would we feel?"

"Well, they didn't," Pamela would reply, and then they would start talking about other things, like the next meeting of the Alfred La Verne Fan Club or whether Miss Leach, the Grade 5 teacher, was in love with Mr. Bradley, the principal.

On the afternoon that It happened, the Pollywog was in jail as usual; and as usual he was trying to escape. For his entire life, which seemed to him to have been very long but was actually only twelve months, he had been staring out at the world from behind bars.

First, there had been the crib in the hospital, into which they had popped him after he was born, and then there was the crib at home. Sometimes they would take

him out of the crib and pop him in the playpen; more bars. The Pollywog would grip the bars, like a convict, and stare out at the world. He would work out elaborate means of escape and sometimes he actually succeeded in escaping. Nobody ever knew how he did it, but the fact was that occasionally he would be discovered outside his playpen or his crib or down off the high chair, which was his third prison.

When the Pollywog did escape he began to crawl at a really unbelievable rate of speed, heading for the open country. (Pamela always said he was trying to get across the Mexican border.) He crawled at a rate of about six miles an hour which meant that you had to run to catch him, and when you caught him he still tried to get away.

On that memorable and hot afternoon, the Pollywog was imprisoned in his high chair having a leisurely late lunch. The high chair had bars on it too – horizontal ones. Also it had a strap which came up between the Pollywog's fat legs and further tethered him to the bars. The Pollywog's agile little brain was ticking like a dollar watch, working on a Grand Escape Plan, while he pretended innocently to eat his Pablum and milk.

As everyone knows, Pablum is the finest food there is for babies. It is chock full of vitamins, rich in calories, jammed with nutriment. And it is so easy to prepare, too! Yum! Yum! Man, oh man!

Everybody knew this except the Pollywog. He liked gum drops, steak, licorice cigarettes and Dr. Kleeb's Pet Food, but he could not stand Pablum.

It was his scheme to get out of the high chair, crawl to the kitchen cupboard, get the door open and steal all the jelly beans which, he happened to know, had been hidden inside. Then he would head for the Mexican border as fast as his four legs would carry him.

He knew the jelly beans were there because he had

seen his mother put them there. Mothers sometimes act as if babies were blind, deaf and dumb. They are anything but. They are a cunning lot; and this one was a master safe-cracker with a brain as sharp as a cold chisel.

Though pretending to eat the Pablum, the Pollywog was really feeding it to Earless Osdick, the black cat who sat directly beneath the high chair. Earless Osdick was the Pollywog's inseparable companion. Grown-ups used to say to each other: "Isn't it touching how the cat follows that child everywhere he goes?" This simply proves they didn't know much about cats.

The reason Earless Osdick followed the Pollywog everywhere and sat so faithfully beneath the high chair was because the Pollywog fed him constantly. Sometimes the Pollywog did it on purpose and sometimes he did it because he wasn't very good at eating. He would miss with his spoon and Earless Osdick would lap up the Pablum as it fell. Earless Osdick loved Pablum. He preferred it to Dr. Kleeb's Pet Food. As for the Pollywog, he liked Earless Osdick to sit under the high chair because, on those occasions when he did escape, he landed on him and the cat cushioned his fall.

Earless Osdick did not know that he was a cat any more than the Pollywog knew that he was a baby. Both of them thought they were dogs and nobody had ever got around to telling them differently.

When Earless Osdick was a kitten he had been brought up with the dog, whose name was Yukon King. Yukon King was perhaps the smallest dog ever born but he did not know that. He thought he was a mastiff or perhaps a malemute, which is a Yukon sled dog. The children had called him Yukon King after the television dog in the Corporal Clancy of the Klondike series and the name had made the dog feel big.

When somebody called "Here, Yukon King!" the dog

27

would dash across the field, feeling fierce, and pretending that he was bounding over the frozen wastes on the trail of desperate criminals. Corporal Clancy was his favourite television program. It was difficult to drag him away from the set for meals if Corporal Clancy was showing. Yukon King would listen for his name and then try to bark in a deep low voice. Actually he had a high, shrill yip but he never stopped practising a deeper bark.

Earless Osdick was called Earless Osdick because he kept his ears folded down like a dog, and not sharply upright like a cat. This is because he slept with the dog, ate with the dog and thought he was a dog. He and Yukon King tried barking daily without much success but they still kept at it.

Actually the Pollywog was much better at barking than either Yukon King or Earless Osdick. He was so convincing that he had once terrified a strange tomcat who had come over to sniff at Earless Osdick. The cat's tail had grown three sizes too big for it and the cat had rushed up a tree in fright. This confirmed the Pollywog in his belief that he was a dog. After all, he walked on four feet, like a dog, and was tied up or locked up like a dog. Sometimes when nobody was looking he ate out of Yukon King's dish, for he was very fond of Dr. Kleeb's Pet Food.

At the moment, the Pollywog was keeping his eye on Mother. Sooner or later, he knew, she would leave the kitchen on some errand and then he would put his Grand Plan into practice.

The only snag in the scheme, as he saw it, was the presence of Peter, in the living room. Peter would tell if he saw him but perhaps Peter would not see him. Peter was absorbed in playing with his cars.

Cars were Peter's life. He usually had one in each

pocket and two in each hand. At the moment he way lying on his back on the sofa, running one of the little cars up and down his leg and over the back of the sofa and making car noises with his mouth.

"B-r-r-r-r-r-r!" went Peter. He was pretending that he was Mr. Whipple the Garbage Man driving a big garbage truck.

"Beep! Beep!" he went. He was pretending that he was in a Crash with another car. Mr. Whipple was killed in the crash. Too bad.

The telephone rang in the hall and Mother left off wiping the dishes and went to answer it. The Pollywog moved like greased lightning. How he escaped from high chairs, playpens and cribs was a secret he never revealed. But the fact is that Mother was no sooner out of the kitchen than *plop!* the Pollywog had landed on Earless Osdick and was halfway toward the jelly beans.

"B-r-r-r-r-r-r!" went Peter, pushing a tiny little fire engine across his knee. Mr. Grimble's Candy Store was burning down but he would put the fire out. Somewhere in the back of his mind he heard a cupboard door open softly. He knew at once which door it was. It was the door of the cupboard where the jelly beans were kept.

Peter was a mild little boy who seldom got into trouble. He lived in a world of his own, surrounded by cars, tractors, fire engines and rocket ships. He could tell a Rambler from a Volkswagen and he knew all about the Boeing 707. When he grew up he intended to be a Garbage Man and take over Mr. Whipple's route when Mr. Whipple was killed in a crash – as he would certainly be.

It would never occur to Peter to open a cupboard door and steal jelly beans or anything else. But when that particular cupboard door did open he was always alert. He

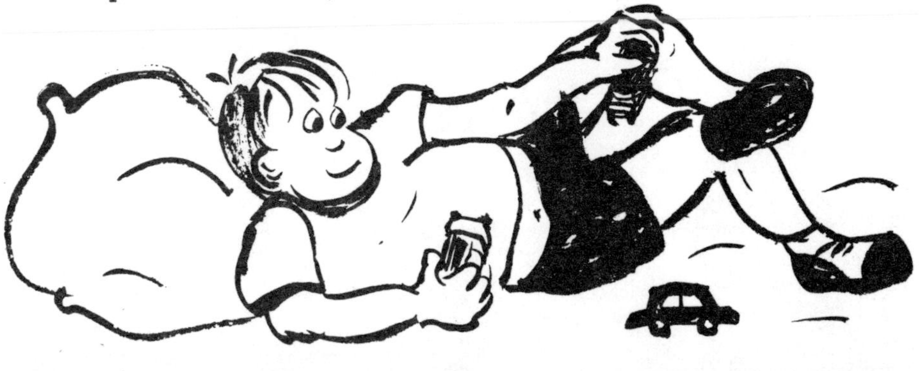

knew its sound as well as he knew his own voice. It was the Goodie Cupboard and when it opened it sometimes meant that his mother was about to give him something sweet.

Peter stuffed all the little cars into the pockets of his shorts, except one – his favourite toy tractor – which he held in his fist. Then he rolled off the sofa and trotted out into the kitchen. There he caught the Pollywog red-handed, with both his forepaws in the jelly bean jar.

The Pollywog's mind was moving at high speed. He realized at once that if his Plan was to succeed the only answer was out-and-out bribery. In a single swift movement he thrust a handful of jelly beans directly at Peter who, without thinking, accepted them.

Peter had never stolen anything in his life. It is true that he had occasionally borrowed little cars from his neighbouring playmates, but that was different. They borrowed cars from him just as frequently and no one really knew or cared who owned what.

But if somebody gives you something can it be called stealing? Peter thought not, though he was wrestling with his conscience. Certainly he was Accepting Stolen Goods, as the police put it, and he knew it. Perhaps if the handful of jelly beans that the Pollywog thrust upon him had not contained three black ones he might have held fast. But, as everybody knows, it is impossible to withstand a black jelly bean for long. Peter began solemnly to inspect one of the black jelly beans and then to sniff it and then to taste it and before he knew it he was eating it. And while he was doing all this, and wrestling with his conscience, the Pollywog was off with his loot and through the hole in the screen door and away for the Mexican border.

He did not get very far, of course. His mother, using that mysterious radar that mothers have, sensed at once

that something was wrong. She dropped the phone, darted out the door, plucked up the Pollywog by his diapers, kicking and struggling, and bore him back into the house. Then she picked up a whistle and blew it as a signal for Penny to come out of the Playhouse.

Penny dropped her book and came running obediently across the field.

"It's Paul again," her mother told her. "I can't keep watching him all the time and get anything done. I found him out in the petunias just now. How he got away I'll never know but he's been at the candy again."

"Poor little Polly," Penny said. "He just hates being cooped up."

"He's slept all morning and he's as frisky as a pup," her mother said. "I want you and Pamela to look after him for the rest of the afternoon. And take Peter with you. He shouldn't be inside on a day like this."

"He just wants to play with his old cars," said Penny. "He's no fun at all."

"Well, go on out to the Playhouse and play Dress-Up," her mother said. "Perhaps Peter will be a Pirate or something. And watch Paul every single minute! Understand, Penny?"

"Yes," said Penny, thinking about Lucy Lawless who had no little brothers to look after.

"Every single minute, mind," her mother said.

"Yes, Mother," said Penny, as she plucked the Pollywog out of her mother's arms. He came quietly now for he knew the jig was up, and besides he liked Penny who usually made a fuss over him. He grinned from ear to ear as she tickled him and then barked twice like a dog. Earless Osdick, who had been mildly stunned when the Pollywog fell on him, heard the bark and padded out obedient-

ly. He had been reviving himself on jelly beans and was now ready for anything.

"Come on, Pete!" Penny called, and Peter, who was back on the sofa playing with his tractor, rolled off and trotted after her.

"I'm in my rocket ship," said Peter. "We're leaving for the moon."

"Don't be so silly, Peter," Penny said, crossly.

"B-r-r-r-r-r!" said Peter, zooming his tractor through the air. "Landing on the moon! Whoosh! Everybody off!"

"What's that black around your lips?" Penny asked suspiciously.

"Don't know," said Peter in a very low voice, meaning he did know.

"It's licorice jelly beans!" cried Penny. "Oh, Peter, you naughty boy – you've been into the jelly beans!"

"Have *not!*" cried Peter, outraged. "Polly gave them to me!"

The Pollywog, hearing his name, barked twice like a dog, opened his fist, and popped the last of the jelly beans into his mouth.

"Just for that you're both going to play Dress-Up with us!" said Penny triumphantly, for she had been looking for an excuse to rope them into it.

"Don't want to," said Peter, as they reached the Playhouse. He didn't like Dress-Up because he always had to dress up as a Lady.

"Pam!" Penny shouted, "go get Patsy. We're all going to play Dress-Up and have a tea party."

"There's no use *asking* Patsy to come," said Pamela, looking up from her comic book. "She's over in the compost heap digging for worms with the Twins – and *they* won't come."

"Well, we'll just have to make her come!" said Penny. "She's supposed to help us look after Polly. Besides we need five if it's going to be any fun."

"I'll tell Patsy she can't come because she painted the windows," Pamela said. "Then she'll *want* to come, and when she starts screaming we'll let her."

She went off to get Patsy, while Penny opened up the Treasure Chest. Keeping one eye on the Pollywog, she began to pull out a series of cast-off evening dresses which had once belonged to her mother and to her various aunts. She held up one particularly elegant dress made of faded green satin with a lace bodice.

"Here, Peter," she said generously, "this is for you."

Peter took it without much enthusiasm.

"Can I still play with my cars?" he asked.

"Oh, Peter!" Penny cried. "Whoever heard of a genteel and refined lady arriving at a tea party and playing with little cars? Really!"

"Just my little dump truck?" Peter said.

"Oh, all right," said Penny.

Across the field she could hear Patsy start to scream. The scream cut the air and just as suddenly stopped. Soon the door burst open and Patsy rushed in, her pigtails flying and her pet snake, Snavely, poking out of the pocket of her jeans.

"It's all so jalopy!" Patsy shouted. "She said I couldn't but I *can*, can't I, Penny?"

"All right," said Penny, remembering Pamela's strategy. "Just this once you can stay to tea."

The three girls each donned a costume from the Treasure Chest.

"I know," Pamela said, "let's pretend this is Pollywog's house and we're all visiting him for tea!"

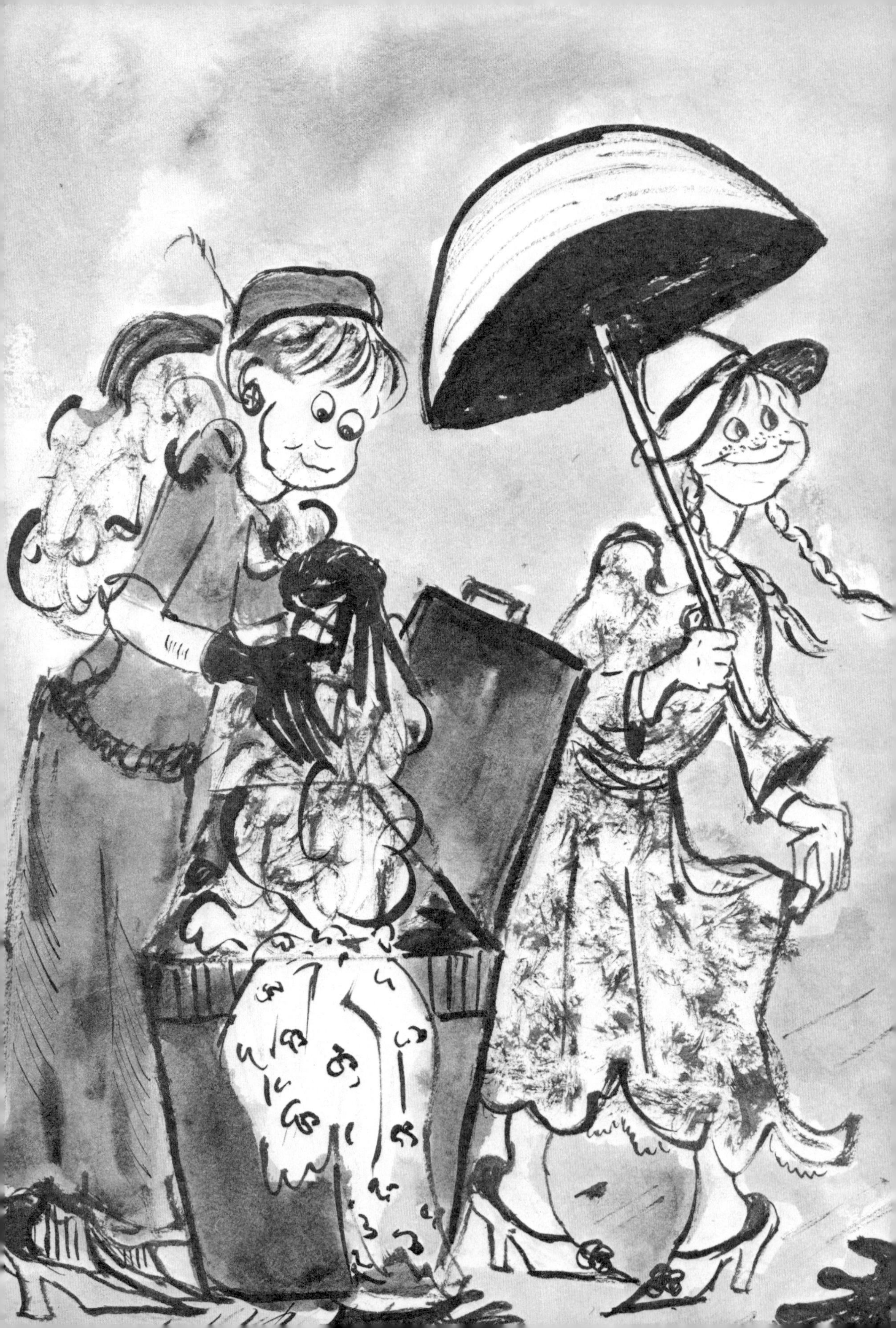

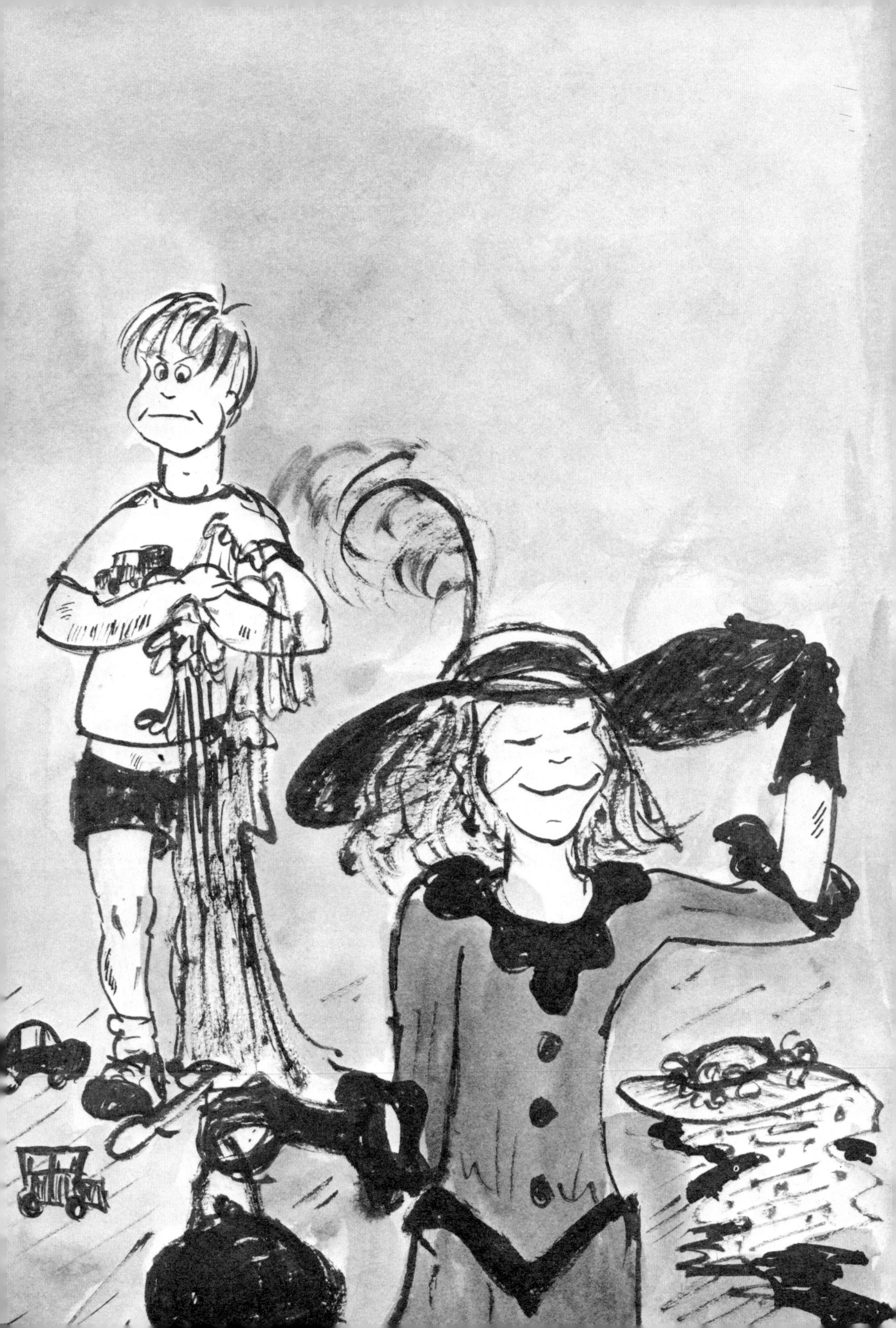

"We'd have to go out and leave him inside alone," said Penny cautiously.

"It would be just for a minute," said Pamela. "See – we pretend it's his bachelor apartment and we all arrive, one after another, and knock on the door and he lets us in and then we sit down and have tea with him."

"He can't," said Patsy. "He's too little."

Penny was thinking. The idea appealed to her but it *would* mean leaving Polly alone for a minute and Mother had said not to take her eyes off him for a single minute.

"But he'll be perfectly safe, Penny," Pamela said. "He *can't* get out of the Playhouse or anything."

"He'll cry if we close the door on him," said Patsy.

"Not if we leave Earless Osdick with him," said Pamela.

"We-ell," said Penny slowly, "I guess nothing could go wrong."

"Paul's the vice-president of the Escapers' Club," said Patsy.

"Well, he can't escape from the Playhouse, stoopid," Pamela said. "Not in one single minute he can't."

"All right," said Penny, "but let's hurry. Everybody dressed? Okay, Polly, you stay here. This is your house, understand? And we're all pretty society ladies coming to tea."

"And you're a bachelor," said Pamela. "And this is really your penthouse apartment."

"We're just going to close the door for a minute, Polly," Penny said. "We'll just walk a bit down the path and come back and you must welcome each of us and offer us tea."

"Or a Martini cocktail," said Patsy.

"Certainly *not!*" said Penny, shocked. "Okay, Polly-woggums? Here – you take Earless Osdick and play with him. We'll be back in a minute." And pushing the others ahead of her she tiptoed out and closed the door.

Once again, the Pollywog found himself in prison with no apparent means of escape. The door was latched and he could not reach the knob. The windows were screened and too high to climb to. The cupboards, which he knew contained little boxes of candy, were also above his reach.

Prisoners flung into dungeon cells in ancient times must have felt the same kind of frustration that the Pollywog felt now.

And then, before his eyes, a miracle occurred.

A square piece in the floor began to rise very slowly. A small green hand appeared and then an arm. A head with two eyes stared out through the opening. Another dog, the Pollywog thought to himself.

But the eyes were not looking at the Pollywog. They were examining Earless Osdick. A second hand appeared, reached out, seized the cat by the nape of the neck, and pulled him down into the blackness.

The piece of floor began to descend back into place again but the Pollywog was quicker than the little green hand. He grabbed the edge of the piece of floor and forced it upward. He shoved his own head into the blackness and then, by dint of squirming, the rest of his body. He could hear a knocking at the door behind him. Suddenly he tumbled down into something dark and as he did he released his grip. The piece of floor snapped back into place and the Playhouse was empty.

This time the Pollywog – for better or for worse – had really escaped.

3/The Adventure Begins

Penny was the first to knock on the Playhouse door. She would pretend that the Pollywog was going to open it and then she would open it herself and let the others in. Then they would all have tea, which was really lemonade, from the small china tea set which sat in one of the Playhouse's small cupboards.

Penny had decided they would open the pretend box of detergent, which contained tiny candies, as a special treat for Peter and the Pollywog (and, if the truth were known, for the others, too).

She knocked three or four times and unlatched the door.

"Here we are, Mr. Pollywog, come to have tea with you," she said, in what she felt was a grown-up voice.

Then she stepped inside.

The Playhouse was quite empty.

"Come on out, you naughty little Polly," Penny said, looking behind the Treasure Chest and under the cot. But there was no sign of the Pollywog or Osdick, and Penny felt a kind of panic rising inside her.

Pamela and the two little ones had followed her into the Playhouse.

"Where's Polly?" Pamela asked.

"I don't know," said Penny, and Pamela could tell that she was on the point of tears. "Honest, Pam, I just don't know!"

"Polly's escaped! Polly's escaped!" cried Patsy in glee, hugging Peter, and the two began to jump up and down shouting "Polly's escaped!"

"Oh, shut up, you two," said Pamela crossly, for she realized the seriousness of it all.

"Well," said Patsy, "I told you they made him vice-president of the Escapers' Club. Now he'll be able to run for president and he'll get in."

"Oh, Pam," Penny said. "We never should have left him – not for a single minute. Mother said so. Now what'll we do?"

"I expect we'd better look for him," Pamela said. "He can't have gone far."

"But how could he get *out?*" Penny said in a shrill voice. "He *couldn't.* We were right outside watching all the time! We'd have *seen* him."

"I expect he went through the trap door," Pamela said, remembering something.

"What trap door?" said Penny. "There *isn't* any trap door and you know it."

"Yes, there is," Pamela said stubbornly. "It's the one the little green man cut with his saw. It probably has hinges on it."

Penny, who had been frantically running about the Playhouse and peering under the chairs and looking out through the curtains and the door, stopped dead.

"What are you talking about, Pam?"

"When we were reading a while ago," said Pamela soberly, "I saw a little saw cut a trap door in the floor, right over there, and I saw a little green man open it and stare at me. Then he went away."

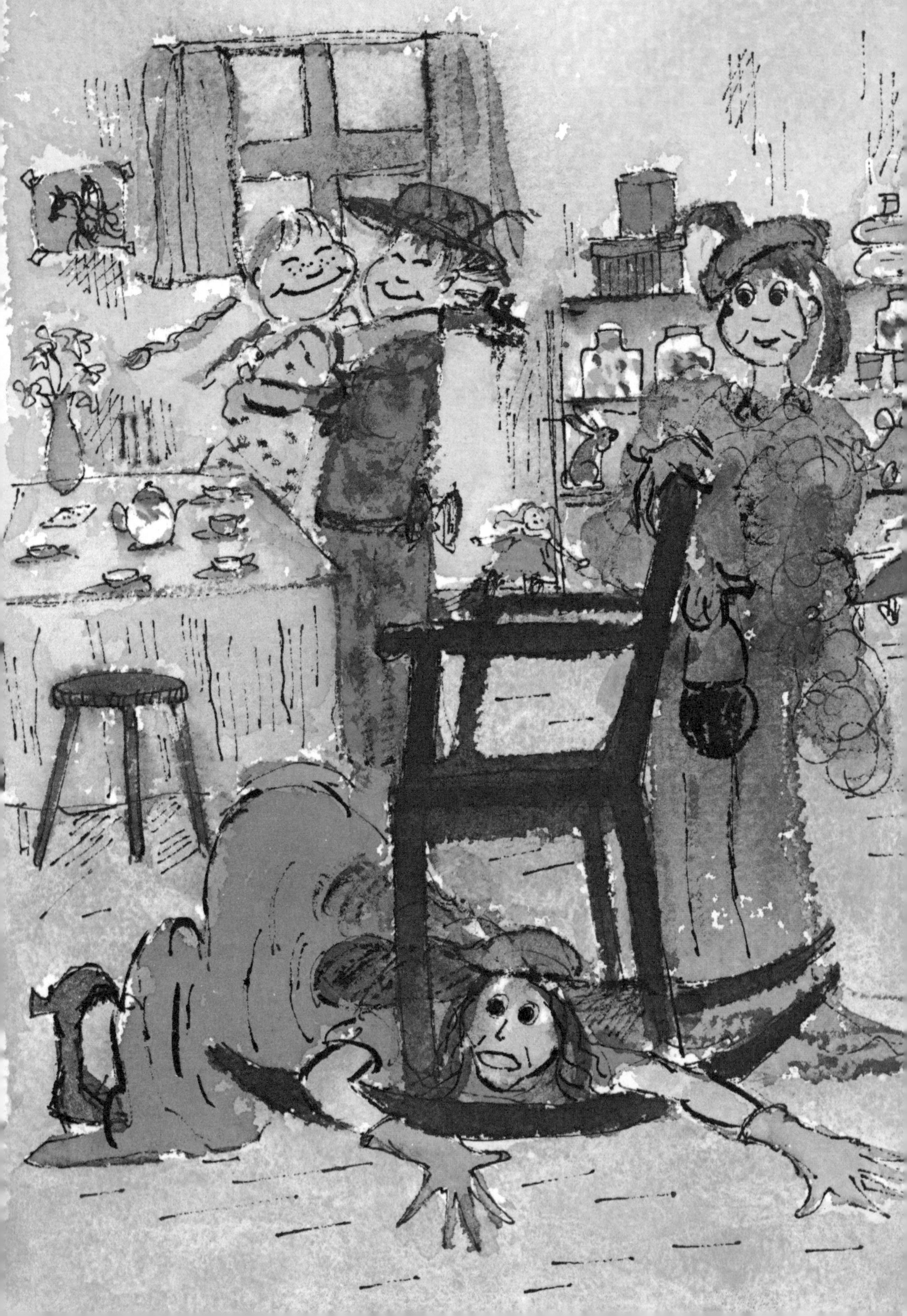

"Pam, you're fibbing!"

"No, I'm not. I saw it. I did too."

"Why didn't you say something?"

"Why should I? Nobody ever believes me when I tell them what I see."

Penny knew this to be true and had no ready answer.

"We'd probably better open the trap door," said Pamela practically, not making any move to do so.

"Don't see any trap door," said Peter.

"I do! I do! I see a little something!" shouted Patsy, dancing about and pointing at a thin line on the floor.

"That's it all right," said Pam nodding her head knowingly.

"Yes," said Penny, who was still a little stunned by it all. "I *do* see it now." She got down on her knees and ran her fingers along the crack in the floor and even picked up some sawdust.

"All right then," she said, pulling herself together and taking charge. "We've got to get it open."

But how? That was the question. There was no handle of any kind to lift; and there was certainly something holding the door where it was. No amount of kicking would cave it in.

"Let's have some tea and discuss it quietly," said Pamela.

"Oh, *Pam*! How could you? With little Polly down there?"

The two older girls began to argue. Peter meanwhile had taken a knife from the knife-fork-and-spoon set that came with the play tea things. With this as a wedge he pried a piece of the linoleum from one edge of the trap door and then poked around between the linoleum and the plywood below until he found what he was looking for. It was a nail that had not been fully driven in.

From his bulging pocket he took out his small tractor.

It had a length of string tied behind it with a loop on the end for pulling things. Peter hooked the loop around the nail head. Then he stood back, let the string tighten and pulled with all his might.

"B-r-r-r-r-r!" said Peter, making tractor noises with his lips. "I'm in my little tractor." For he always imagined that he himself was at the controls of any of the toy cars that he was manipulating at the moment.

"Look, Penny!" squealed Patsy. "Pete's really smart! He really is!"

The trap door was slowly opening, on little hinges, just as Pamela had guessed.

"Oh, Peter!" cried Penny. "I could just hug you."

"He's the president of the Tractor Club!" shouted Patsy.

"Can I have a little candy now?" said Peter. He knew that he had done something quite noble and felt that he ought to have a prize.

"Take the whole box," said Penny generously.

Peter took the candies and was about to cram a handful into his mouth when he remembered his manners and passed them all around. Everybody had a candy and everybody felt a little better.

Then all four got down on their knees and stared into the black hole that had opened up beneath the Playhouse.

"Polly?" shouted Penny. "Polly? Are you down there?"

No answer. Not even an echo.

"Woof! Woof!" barked Patsy. She did it extremely well but there was still no answer.

"Penny, get a rock and drop it down," Pamela suggested. "We can tell how far down it is when we hear it land."

"*I* will!" squealed Patsy. She rushed out the door and returned in an instant, with several rocks of various sizes.

She dropped one in and heard it make a satisfying PLOP almost at once.

"It can't be very far to the bottom," Penny said. "Pete, drop your tractor down on the string and see if you can feel anything."

Peter unhooked his tractor from the nail on the trap door and suspended it into the gloom, reaching as far down as he could.

"Touched something," he said.

"Pull it up!"

Peter hauled the tractor up. It had sand on its wheels.

"It can't be very far down," said Penny.

"Somebody's going to have to go down there," said Pamela a little uncertainly.

"I will! I will!" squealed Patsy, who was known in the family as The Volunteer. She had clambered halfway into the darkness when Penny pulled her back.

"No you *won't*, Patsy," she said firmly. "It's up to me."

It took a great deal of courage for Penny to say this, for she was mortally afraid of what lay below. Pamela's story of the mysterious trap door and the strange little man who was coloured green, the Pollywog's absolute disappearance, the darkness and the mystery – all these things terrified her.

She was so scared she was trembling but all the same she knew she must go for she was the oldest and she was the one responsible for Paul. She would have to set an example to the other children who instinctively followed her lead. If anybody else was going to get swallowed up or captured by Green People, then she would have to be the one. If she did not take the lead now, she knew she would be sorry for it all her life.

"Yes – come on back, Patsy," said Pamela, understanding everything clearly. "Penny has to go."

Penny swung herself over the side of the pit, holding on to the edge of the Playhouse floor with her hands. For a moment she clung there, a thin frightened little girl in an old discarded evening dress, holding her lips tightly together to keep her teeth from chattering. Then she let go and the other children could hear a KLUMPH! as she hit the bottom.

"Are you all right, Penny?" Pamela called down.

"I think so," came the answer. "It's sort of sandy. I'm going to feel around."

They could hear her moving around below, in the darkness, and then they heard her voice, hollow in the gloom, call upward again in excitement.

"There are little steps here! They go down! I'm going to follow them down . . ."

"Wait, Penny," Pamela called. "We'll all come. It'll be a lot safer."

She could almost hear Penny thinking about this in the dark below.

"All right, then," Penny said, for she desperately wanted company. "Let the little ones down first and you bring up the rear." It was a phrase taken from *Lucy Lawless, Girl Pirate*: "Let the prisoners go first, Cap'n, and you bring up the rear."

"Maybe we ought to take Yukon King," Patsy said. "He's never had a real adventure. It would do him good."

"He could *pertect* us," Peter said soberly. He was the only one, besides Yukon King, who really believed in Yukon King's invincibility.

"I don't s'pose it would hurt," said Pamela.

"I'll get him!" Patsy squealed and rushed off to the big elm tree where Yukon King could always be found asleep on a hot afternoon.

"Wait, Penny," Pamela called. "We're going to bring Yukie."

Yukon King (who very much disliked being called "Yukie") was at that moment lying flat on his back with his tiny paws in the air, snarling in his sleep. He was re-dreaming an episode from Corporal Clancy of the Klondike, which he had seen on TV the previous Monday. He had just reached the part where Corporal Clancy, bound hand and foot by The Bonanza Bandit, is saved by his faithful and incredibly intelligent malemute (played by Yukon King). Then Patsy woke him up by rolling him over.

Yukon King bounded high into the air, and, with his back to the tree, bared his teeth preparing to meet all comers. Then he saw Patsy, dropped the role of malemute, and crawled up to her wiggling his little behind.

"C'mon, Yukon King," said Patsy, being careful to address him formally because of the importance of the occasion. "We're going on an adventure and you're going to protect us."

The effect of this speech on the little dog was electric. He puffed out his tiny chest, raised his head in the air and began to strut toward the Playhouse, fairly bursting with pride. Patsy had been right. An adventure – *any* adventure – would do him good.

"We'd best drop him down first," said Pamela, as the two arrived back. She picked up Yukon King and held him over the abyss. He didn't like it a bit and was about to yelp in terror, but thought better of it. If he showed fear they mightn't take him at all. Pamela dropped him and Penny caught him in her arms and Yukon King was so grateful to find a friend below that he slobbered all over her.

"All right, Peter, over you go," Pamela said.

"Wait," said Peter, retrieving his tractor and stuffing it in his pocket. Then he jumped down quickly and Penny caught him. Patsy came next in an enthusiastic bound. "It's so *jalopy*," she whispered to Peter and the two hugged each other with excitement and delight.

"Come on, Pam," Penny called. But Pamela was not to be hurried. Very slowly and very methodically she closed the Playhouse door. She looked about and picked up as many of the little boxes of candies as the pockets of her shorts would hold. Then she carefully slung herself over the edge and dropped down.

The adventure had begun.

4/The Mysterious River

"The stairs are just over here," Penny said, in a whisper. She didn't know why she was whispering, but it seemed appropriate.

"Everybody touch hands now," she said. "I'll carry Yukie under my arm so he won't get lost. Patsy behind me, then Peter, and Pam at the rear."

In the shaft of pale light cast by the opening in the Playhouse above, the children could see that they were in a sort of cave. Directly ahead of them and leading downward were the stairs that Penny had found. They certainly weren't much; nothing more than crude steps dug out of the clay and sand.

And so they started down them, a step at a time, Penny in the lead. She was not frightened any longer. She felt instead a kind of thrill at leading a real expedition into the "bowels of the earth" (a phrase she had picked up from *Lucy Lawless, Girl Sandhog*). For the first time in her life she was completely on her own, with lives perhaps dependent upon her. It steadied her and she felt herself almost growing taller as a result of it.

She put out one foot very carefully after each step to make sure that there *was* another. The little tunnel, down which the steps led in a gentle incline, was quite narrow and the sides were wet and slippery. Long roots poked

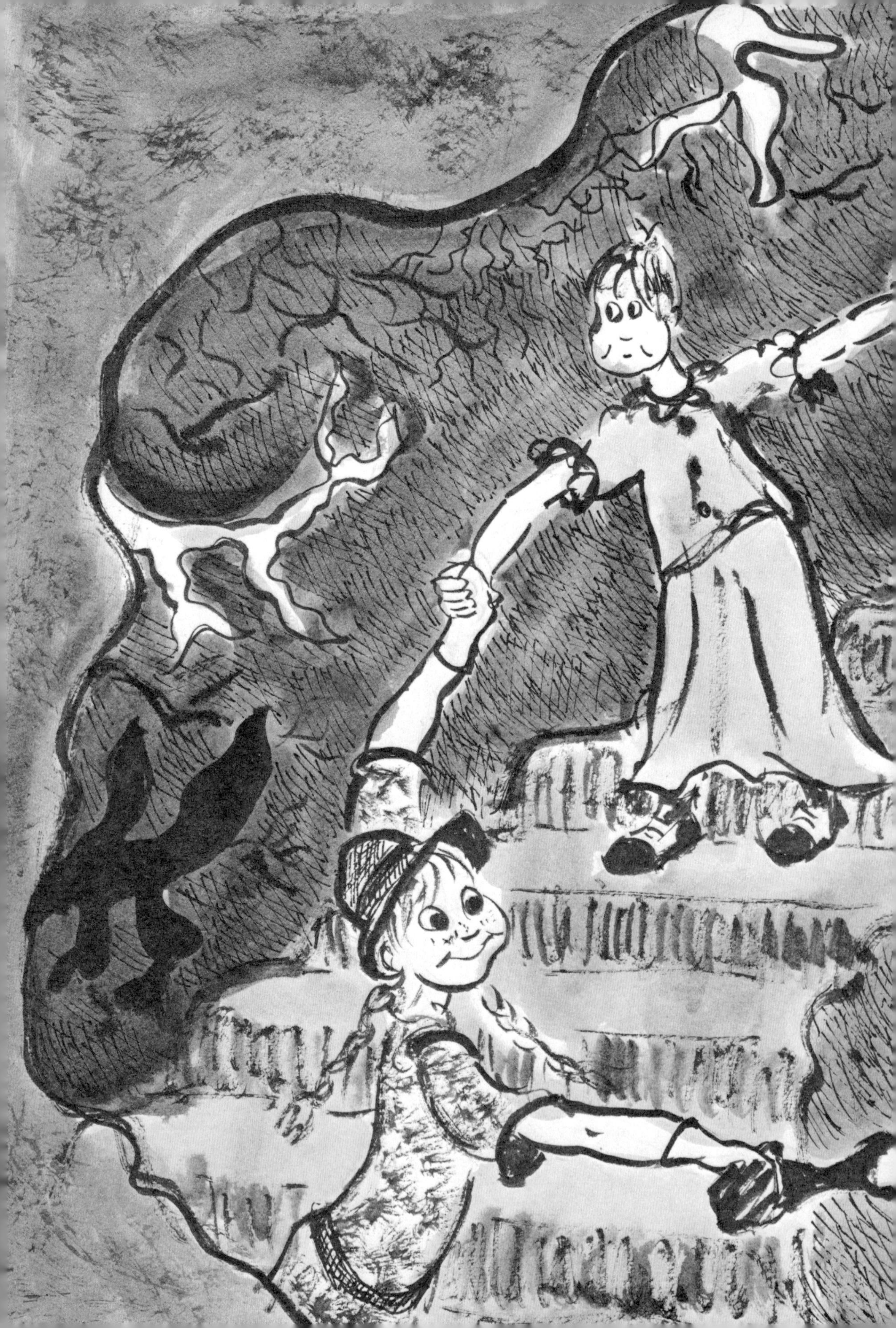

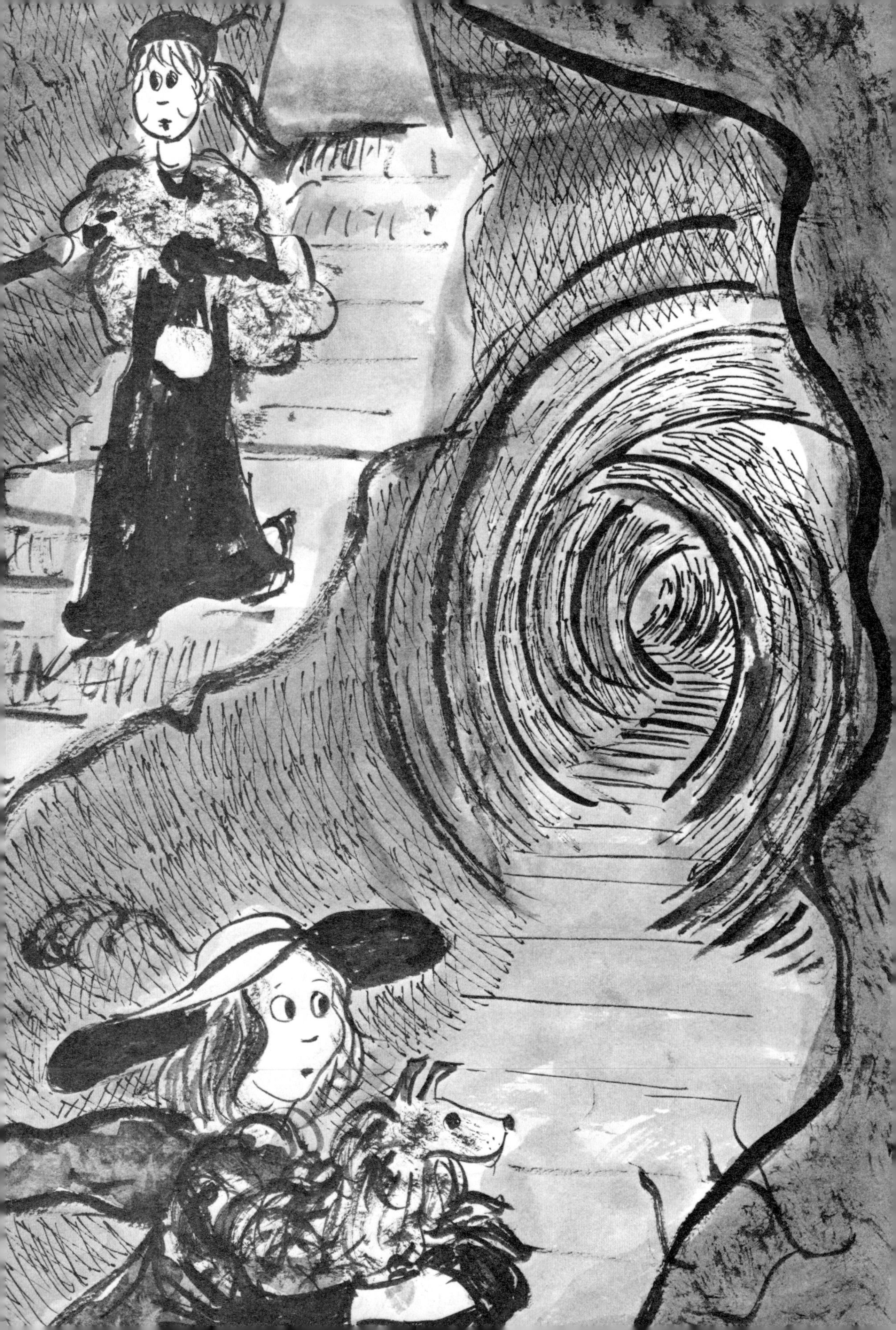

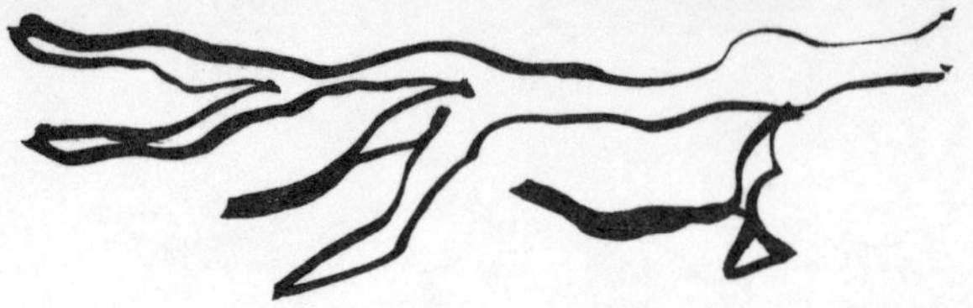

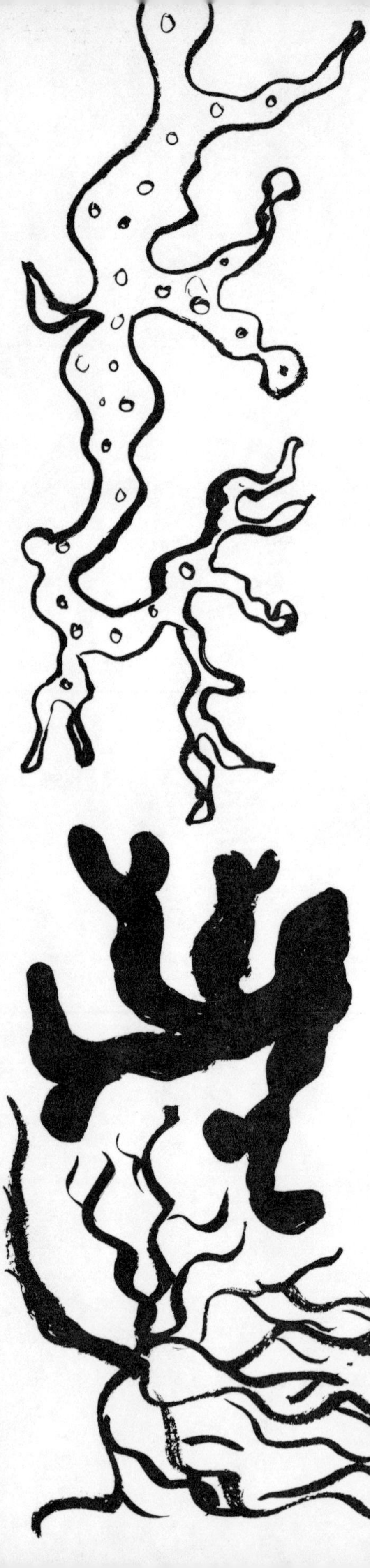

through them and Penny realized that they must be the tap roots of trees growing in the world above. Indeed, there were roots everywhere: some like long, wriggling snakes, slender and sinuous, others like short fat sausages with small bulbets on the ends, some intertwined like spaghetti or matted and woven together like fish nets, some like thin white worms coiling this way and that, and others as thick as a man's wrist branching down through the roof like inverted trees and continuing into the very floor of the tunnel down which the children were clambering. It was as if they were advancing deep into a ghostly and sunless forest; and that is what it was, of course: the underside of the forest above, which few people ever see.

Patsy, who could count to a hundred and was proud of it, was counting the steps. She had reached seventy-three when suddenly, down ahead of them, Penny became aware of a kind of glow.

"There's something ahead!" she called back to Pamela. "Everybody stop."

Peter took one of the little cars out of his pocket and began to run it along the side of the tunnel.

"B-r-r-r-r-!" he said. "I'm in my bulldozer, breaking up the ground."

"Be *quiet*, Peter!" Penny said in a sharp whisper. "We don't know what's below. Now listen, everybody: we must move very quietly and carefully. There might be somebody or something below that wants to hurt us. We mustn't let them know we're here. No more counting, Patsy, and Pete, you put that car away."

They moved on down toward the pale, glowing light, sliding soundlessly over the soft clay steps. The tunnel began to widen out and suddenly there were no more steps and no more tunnel.

The children stood for a moment in the silence, awed

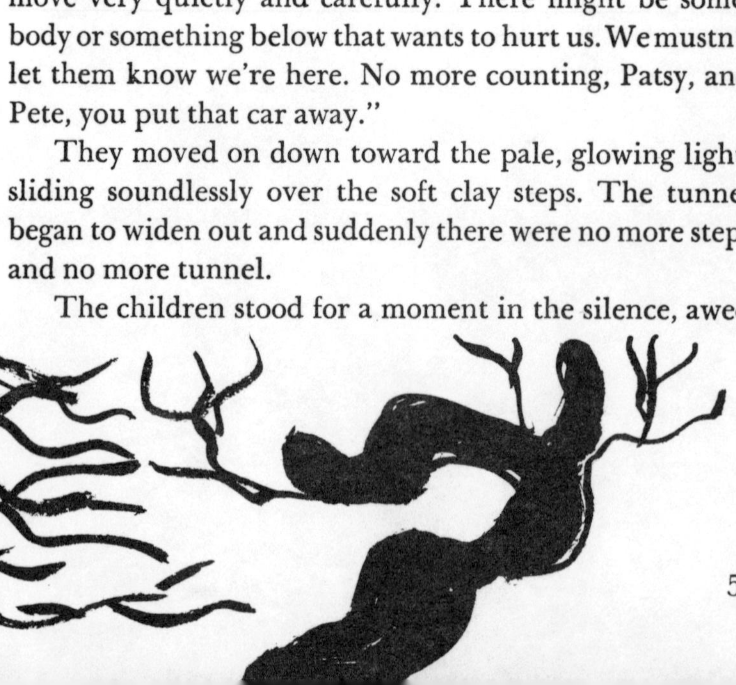

by what they saw. They seemed to be in an enormous cavern so huge that they could not see the far side, so high they could scarcely see the roof. Through the cavern wound a river, like a bright, shimmering serpent. It glowed and sparkled and this glow was reflected in hundreds of pinpoints of light from the crystal rocks all around. It was the river itself that seemed to supply the soft light – a sort of twilight to which the children quickly grew accustomed. After a few moments they were easily able to pick out the various objects in the cavern: the shapes of boulders on the far side of the river, the dark walls that rose above them, and the "icicles," as Patsy called them, which hung from the ceiling, flashing and glittering in the reflected glow of the river.

"Oh!" said Pamela, clapping her hands in delight, "It's so pretty!" And indeed it was – beautiful, strange, and mysterious.

Patsy rushed to the edge of the river and Penny caught her just in time. The trick of the moment, she knew, was to try to keep Patsy from falling in. Patsy seldom got within hailing distance of a river or lake or a pond or a puddle without falling in.

"What should we do now, Penny?" Pamela asked. "There's no sign of the Pollywog – or anybody else for that matter."

"We'll have to explore a way along the river bank, I guess," Penny said.

"Yes, but which way – up or down?"

Penny thought hard about that one.

"I know," Pamela said. "Some of us could go one way and some the other."

The idea of separating into two groups did not appeal to Penny.

"We could take off the Dress-Up clothes and pile them

here," Pamela said. "It's awfully hot anyway. Then Pete and I could walk five hundred steps down the river and you and Patsy five hundred steps the other way. If we find anything we bark like Pollywog does. If we don't we come back and meet here."

It seemed logical enough, Penny agreed, and so they shed their Dress-Up clothes and headed out in couples, in their shorts or jeans and T-shirts. Penny was glad now that Pamela was along. Her calmness and logic helped to steady her. Privately she decided that Pam could have half the Playhouse when they got back.

Penny had barely gone three hundred steps up the river when she heard Pamela bark. Yukon King bristled at the sound and Penny let him down. She and Patsy ran after him and quickly caught up with Pamela and Peter.

Pamela was holding up a shoe.

"It's Polly's," she said. "You know how he's always trying to get them off. He hates shoes."

"Then it's settled," Penny said. "We have to go in this direction down river."

"What about the Dress-Up clothes?" Patsy asked.

"We leave them here," Penny said firmly. "They'd only be an encumbrance." She rolled the big word around on her tongue, proud of having used it correctly.

They set off again, following the bank of the gently flowing river.

"Look – what's that?" said Pamela, pointing out into the water.

"Where?"

"There – that thing that looks like a pipe."

"It *is* a pipe," said Peter.

And it certainly seemed to be: a thin metal pipe coming down from the high ceiling of the glowing cavern and into the river.

"It's just like the pipes our taps are on," Patsy said.

"Oh, Patsy, you've figured it out," Pamela said. "It must be the well! Father always said that we must get our water from an underground river or lake or something."

"Then we're right under the well," said Penny, marvelling. "So at least we know where we *are* – sort of. Come on, we've got to find Polly."

They trudged on for several minutes but then they came up hard against a stone wall. This was the limit of the great cavern. The river now entered a dark tunnel.

"Whatever are we going to do now?" said Penny.

"Build a boat," said Peter, the practical.

"We can't. There isn't a stick of wood or anything else that I can see."

"Here's something," said Peter, reaching down.

He picked up a small toy boat, made of wood, the paint faded and the hull chipped.

"Why, it's my little sailboat," he said. "The one I lost."

Now that's strange, Penny thought. How could *that* have got down here?

"Somebody's been playing with my sailboat!" Peter muttered. "They've broken the mast!"

It was at this exact moment that Patsy, true to form, fell in with a splash.

She was up in a moment, swimming like an eel, but for the wrong side, having lost her bearings in the plunge. Patsy had been the first of the children to learn to swim, just as she was the first in many things that required agility. Most important of all, she had been the first to learn to cross her eyes, a feat which was greatly admired by the others but which sometimes unnerved old gentlemen. They would pat the child on the head and remark on her large and beautiful brown eyes, whereupon Patsy would look up with an angelic smile and cross both eyes so that

they almost vanished into the bridge of her nose. It usually upset people when she did this, but then Patsy rather enjoyed upsetting people.

Falling into rivers, of course, held no terrors for her. It happened almost daily. She swam quickly across and hauled herself, dripping, onto the far bank. She looked around for the others and not finding them burst into tears at once.

"Over here, silly!" Penny shouted at her. "You went the wrong way."

Patsy stopped crying as quickly as she had begun, jumped back into the water and proceeded to swim toward the children. Halfway across she stopped swimming and stood up.

"Why, the water only comes to her waist," said Penny.

"I see a little light!" Patsy chirped at her.

"Where, Patsy?"

"In the tunnel – way down the river."

"Come on," Penny said quickly. "I believe we can all wade it. Pam, you better carry Yukon King."

But Yukon King had already plunged into the water and was swimming strongly toward Patsy.

"Make a human chain," Penny said, as she reached Patsy. "Now everybody hold hands tightly and we'll walk down the river together through the tunnel. It's really quite warm, isn't it?"

And it was – quite warm and pleasant. The water glowed all around them and Penny noticed that when it rolled off them each drop seemed to glitter briefly.

Thus they entered the tunnel at the end of which could be seen a pinpoint of light, just as Patsy had reported. But they were scarcely in the tunnel before a weird and hollow cry, far off in the distance, echoed up toward them.

"There's something in the tunnel," Pamela whispered.

54

"It's a ghost," said Peter.

The children stopped and clung together. The sound stopped, then began again. It sounded something like "OG" repeated over and over again.

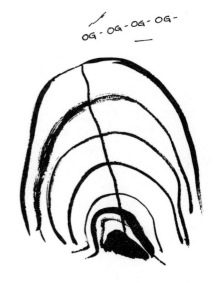

"I don't want to go!" said Patsy, looking as if she were going to burst into tears once more.

"Be quiet," whispered Penny, "and listen!" She could feel her own heart pounding and her knees knocking together but she had no intention of turning back. The Pollywog was her responsibility and he must be found. She listened for the sound and it came again, in waves, echoing off the walls of the dark wet tunnel — "OG!-OG-og-og-og . . ."

"It sounds a lot like people talking," said Pamela. "You know, like they were in another room."

"There must be somebody at the far end of the tunnel," Penny whispered.

"Maybe they've got Polly," Peter said, pushing his newly found boat around in the water and making small tooting noises under his breath.

"Sshsh!" Penny cautioned him. She listened again but now the great tunnel was absolutely quiet. She gripped Patsy tightly by one arm, to prevent her from turning back in panic, and then began moving cautiously forward again.

"Stick close to the wall, everybody," she whispered, and the children, up to their waists in water, crept forward.

As they moved on they could see the light at the end of the tunnel growing larger and larger and brighter and brighter. The softly flowing waters rustled past them, moving in the same direction.

Pamela, who noticed almost everything, and whose large eyes had been peering solemnly about, now saw that a narrow ledge, about the width of one person, ran along the side of the tunnel and just above the surface of the water. She climbed up onto it at once and the others followed her, creeping forward in single file.

"Something touched me!" said Peter suddenly.

Penny put her hand quickly over Patsy's mouth to stop her from screaming. Patsy was fond of screaming and quite often screamed at the top of her voice when she had no reason to. When she was frightened she *really* screamed and she was frightened now.

"It's trying to steal my boat!" cried Peter, outraged.

Penny's eyes widened: in the gloom she saw that a small green arm had come out of the water and seized Peter's boat.

"Give me my boat!" said Peter, hitting at something under the water. He disliked it very much when another child tried to take one of his toys by force. This wasn't exactly a child, perhaps; he didn't really know *what* it was. But the principle was the same.

"Grab it, Pam!" cried Penny, letting go of Patsy and making a dive at the green arm. She caught something slithery and hung on; Peter was still punching away with his small fists and Pamela was now helping as best she could. Behind her, Penny could hear Patsy start to scream.

The three of them managed to haul from the water a small green-coloured person with large floppy ears, great staring eyes and a sharp little nose. He had no hair to speak of and wasn't much more than two feet high. In spite of his size, he was terribly strong. It took the three of them to hold him and even then it was a struggle. The little man rolled his eyes horribly and bared his sharp, lizard-like teeth as he threshed about in their grip.

"Shouldn't steal toys," said Peter in a grieved voice, trying to wedge the boat out of the green man's hand. But the little man clung to it with a steady grip.

"Well, I guess you can play with it for a while," Peter said. "But give it back after."

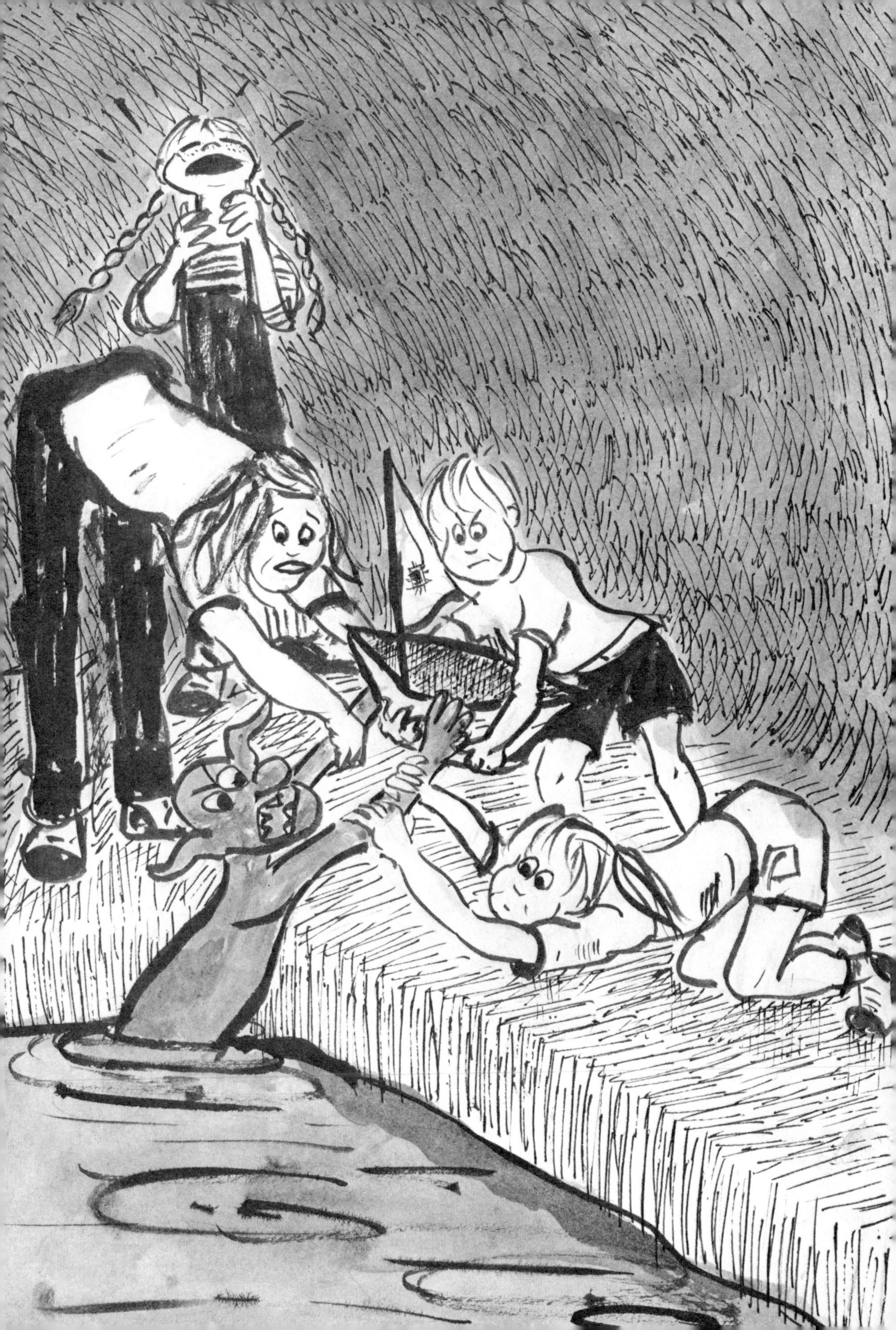

The little man hissed at him, like a kitten caught in a corner.

"Oh, do shut up, Peter," said Penny. "Can't you see he's scared?"

"I'm scared too," said Patsy, who had stopped screaming.

"What's your name?" Peter asked curiously. "I'm Peter," he added, amiably, for he was not a boy who could hold a grudge for long.

"Og," said the green man.

"Hi, Og!" said Peter.

"Never mind names," said Penny, more grimly. She poked the green man in his stomach. "What have you done with my little brother?"

The little person stared at her balefully.

"Og?" it asked.

"You've stolen our baby brother – don't try to deny it!" Penny said, tightening her grip on his arm and poking him again. "Where is he? We want him back."

"It's my turn to play with the boat, Og," Peter said, reaching for the toy.

"Og," said the little green man suddenly. "Og *Og* Og-Og." He clung fiercely to the boat.

"I believe the only word he knows is 'Og,'" said Pamela, slowly.

"Maybe he's not growed yet," said Peter.

"Maybe they only *have* one word," said Pamela, thinking about it to herself.

"Silly!" said Peter. "Whoever heard of just *one* word?"

"We aren't getting anywhere," said Penny. "And we've made an awful lot of noise. Unless we think of a plan, we're going to be in trouble."

"What about Og?" said Pamela.

"He's not much use with his one word," said Penny.

"But what do we *do* with him?"

"Tie him up!" said Penny, coming to a quick decision. "We can't take him with us and we can't let him escape to warn any others like him. Here, Peter, give me that string of yours."

With Pamela's help she turned the protesting Og over on his stomach and then, pushing up his legs behind him and pinning his arms back around them, she neatly tied his thumbs together. The method had been carefully explained, with diagrams, in a clever book called *One Hundred Things a Child Can Do on a Rainy Afternoon.* She and Pamela had known it would come in handy sometime and had practised it many times on whichever one of the Terrible Twins they could catch and hold down long enough.

"Now," said Penny, "here's what we'll do first: I'll sneak forward along the ledge to the end of the tunnel and have a look. The rest of you stay here and wait till I get back. Pamela – you're in charge. Keep Patsy quiet and make sure Og doesn't wriggle free."

The green man, lying helpless on his stomach, was slithering about on the ledge muttering to himself over and over again in a small tortured voice. Peter had to keep pushing him back against the wall to prevent him falling into the water.

"Be careful, Penny," whispered Pamela and she squeezed her older sister's hand – something she had very rarely done before in her life.

Penny squeezed back and then began to move stealthily forward, half crouching as she went. Pamela watched as her thin figure, silhouetted against the light at the end of the tunnel, became smaller and smaller and then, at last, vanished into the gloom – into the Unknown.

She and Peter and Patsy sat on the edge of the ledge,

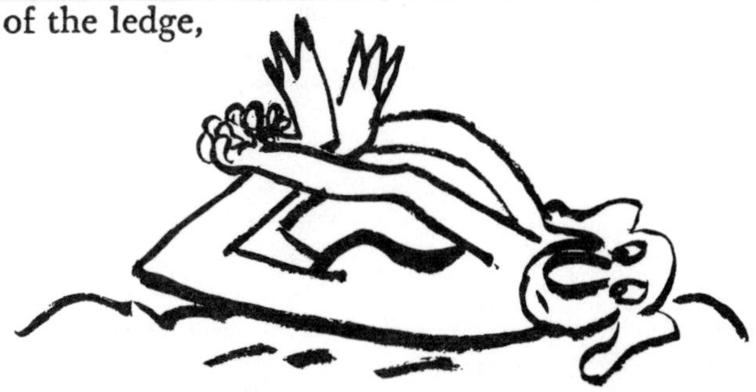

dangling their feet in the water, and settled down to wait.

And they waited . . . and waited . . . and waited; but there was no sign and no word from Penny. She did not come and she did not call. And now the silence in the great gloomy tunnel was oppressive: for there was no human sound at all – only the whisper of the breeze whistling down the long tunnel . . . only the sighing of the luminous river as it slipped past the dark rocks.

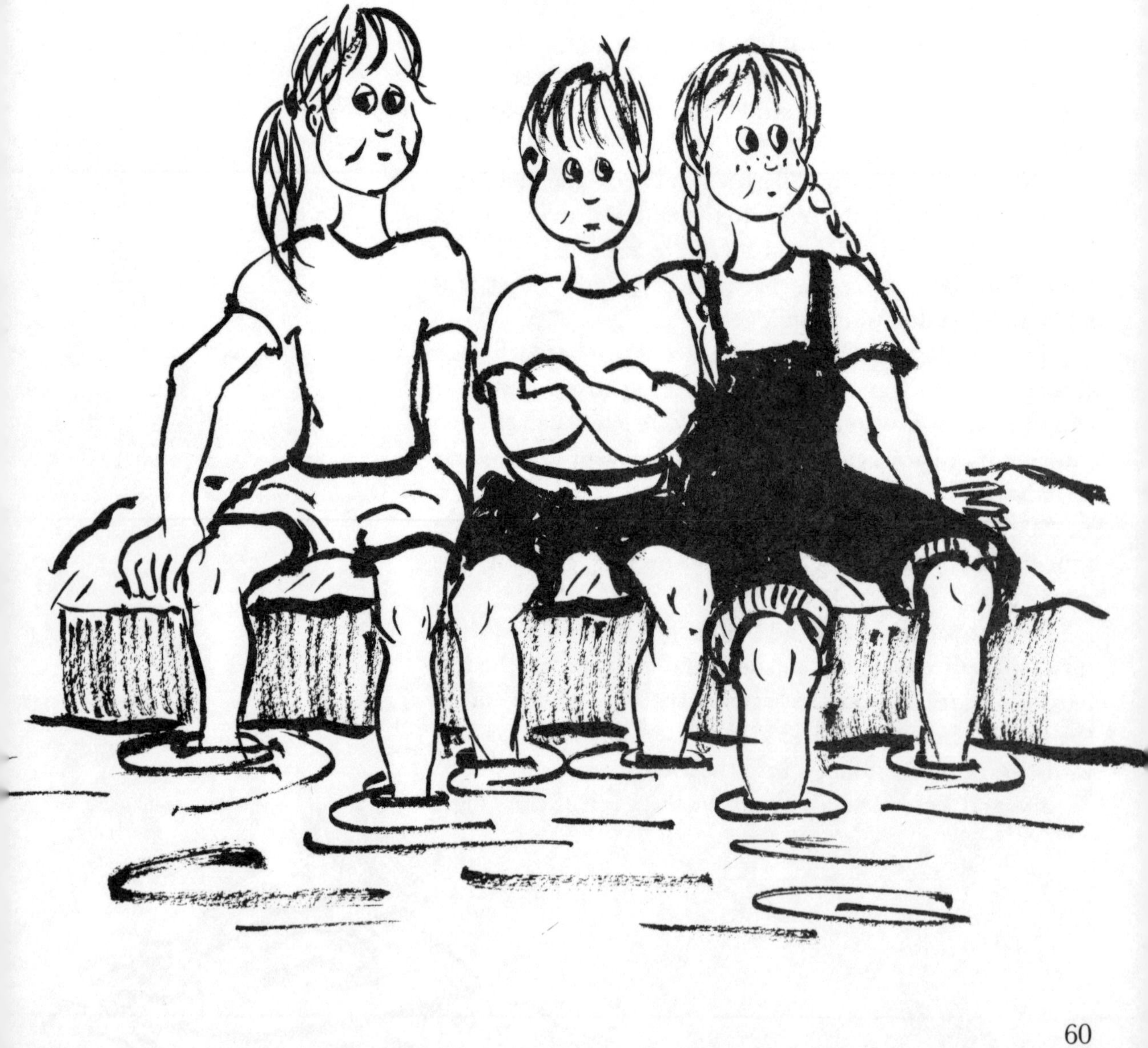

5/The Secret World of Og

Penny had moved several hundred yards in a crouching position, trying her best to hold her breath, when something stopped her. She saw at once that it was a kind of crude net strung across the river and fastened to the ledge. At the edges, in the half-light, she saw several little boats tied to it. They were made of some soft, porous material, but there was no sign of life.

Ahead she could hear a roar of water.

"Why, that would be a waterfall," she thought. "That's why the net is here – of course! To prevent the boats going over."

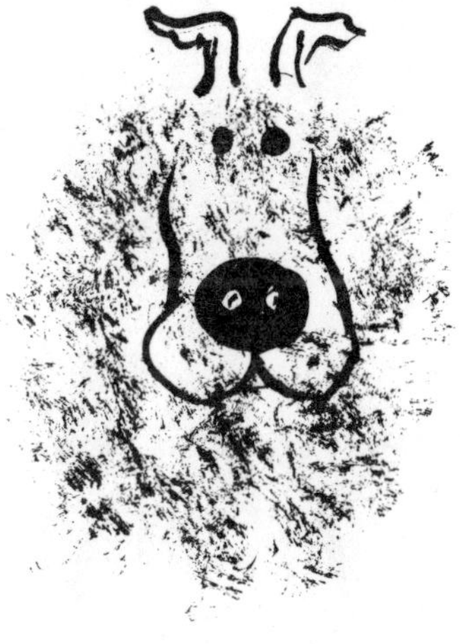

Something wet and cold and clammy touched her leg and she jumped straight up stifling a scream. To her relief she saw that it was only Yukon King's nose. The dog had followed her along the stony ledge.

"Why, Yukie," said Penny, marvelling, "I do believe you mean to protect me after all."

Yukon King looked very pleased at that.

Penny climbed easily over the net, heaving Yukon King over with her, and, staying carefully on the ledge, crept to the tunnel's outlet.

Directly below her, the river poured out of the cavern's black mouth and tumbled in a long slender cataract,

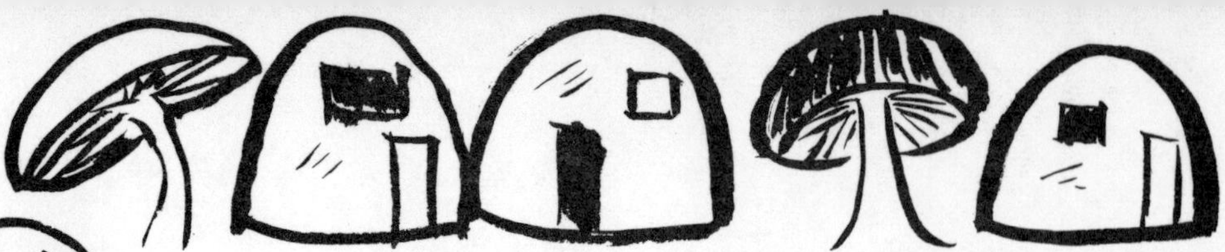

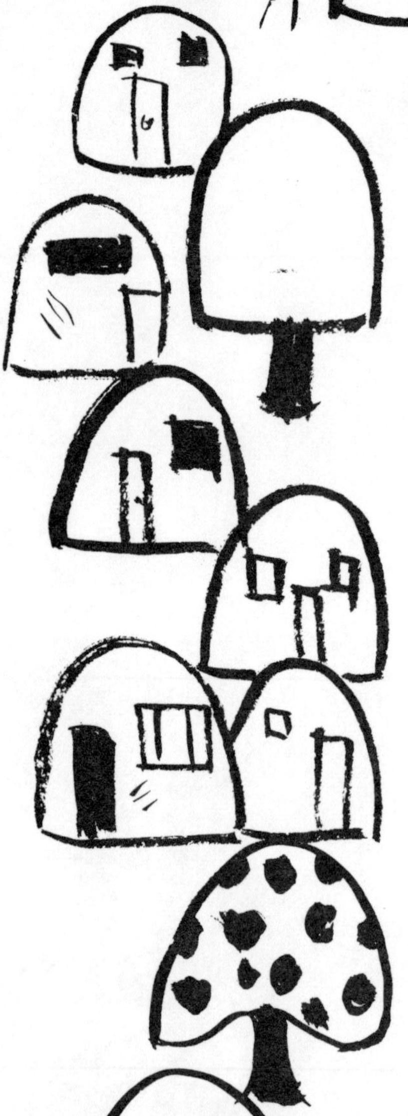

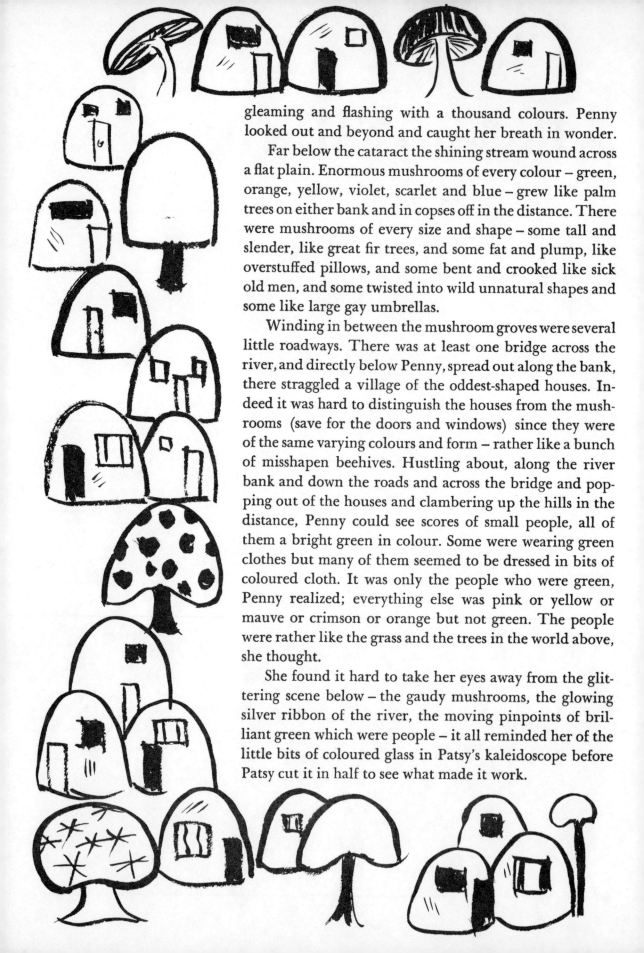

gleaming and flashing with a thousand colours. Penny looked out and beyond and caught her breath in wonder.

Far below the cataract the shining stream wound across a flat plain. Enormous mushrooms of every colour – green, orange, yellow, violet, scarlet and blue – grew like palm trees on either bank and in copses off in the distance. There were mushrooms of every size and shape – some tall and slender, like great fir trees, and some fat and plump, like overstuffed pillows, and some bent and crooked like sick old men, and some twisted into wild unnatural shapes and some like large gay umbrellas.

Winding in between the mushroom groves were several little roadways. There was at least one bridge across the river, and directly below Penny, spread out along the bank, there straggled a village of the oddest-shaped houses. Indeed it was hard to distinguish the houses from the mushrooms (save for the doors and windows) since they were of the same varying colours and form – rather like a bunch of misshapen beehives. Hustling about, along the river bank and down the roads and across the bridge and popping out of the houses and clambering up the hills in the distance, Penny could see scores of small people, all of them a bright green in colour. Some were wearing green clothes but many of them seemed to be dressed in bits of coloured cloth. It was only the people who were green, Penny realized; everything else was pink or yellow or mauve or crimson or orange but not green. The people were rather like the grass and the trees in the world above, she thought.

She found it hard to take her eyes away from the glittering scene below – the gaudy mushrooms, the glowing silver ribbon of the river, the moving pinpoints of brilliant green which were people – it all reminded her of the little bits of coloured glass in Patsy's kaleidoscope before Patsy cut it in half to see what made it work.

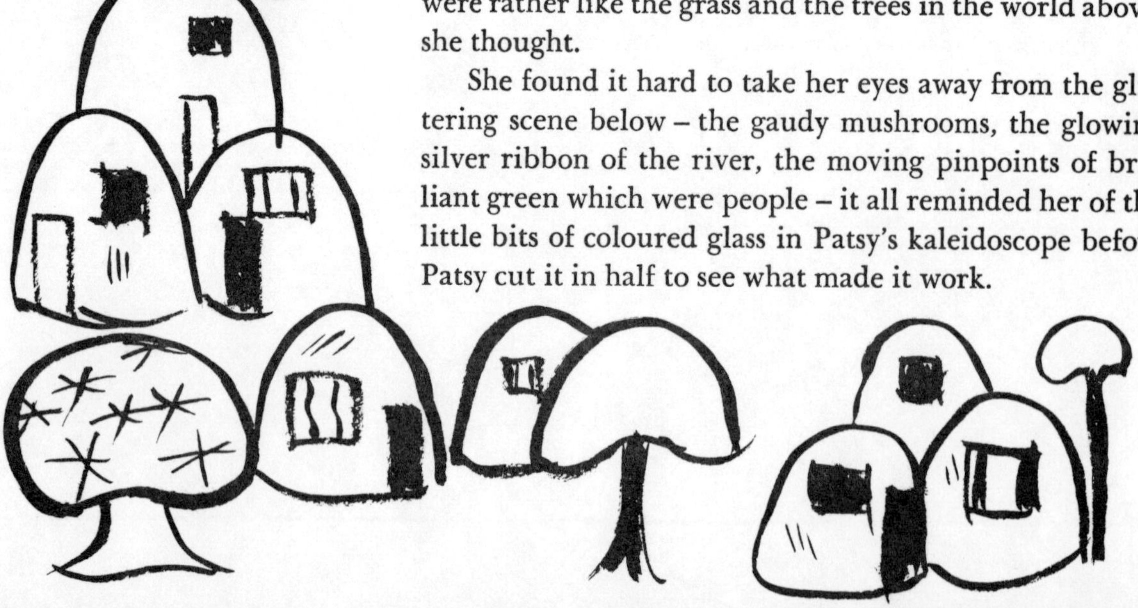

Penny had no doubt at all that the Pollywog was down there somewhere. But where? And who were these people who lived far below the earth in a weird mushroom world? Why had they taken Polly down below anyway? And what was the reason for those little steps leading directly up to the Playhouse?

"Why, it's just like one of Pam's silly comic books," she said to herself. And all at once, as she looked down again on the scene below, Penny could see why Pamela always laughed at the unbelievable comic book stories. In spite of herself and in spite of the seriousness of the situation, she found herself giggling. It was just too silly for words! It must be a dream, like *Alice in Wonderland!* She pinched herself and was convinced that it didn't hurt a bit.

So it was a dream after all! She felt vaguely disappointed at that and wondered whether she should wake up and have some cookies and milk or keep on for a while.

But at that moment she felt a second pinch that hurt so much she screamed in pain. She looked down and saw that a small green hand had seized her by the forearm in a grip as tight as a vise. Then she knew that she wasn't dreaming.

"Let go!" cried Penny, instinctively. She twisted around and saw a tiny green man about two and a half feet high, with big staring eyes and huge floppy ears. He held her arm quite tightly and obviously had no intention of letting go.

Penny felt herself shiver again with fear. The green man peered straight into her face and she could see the staring whites of his eyes, his leathery green skin, as smooth and shiny as a frog's, and his sharp, pointed teeth.

He had come up very softly and quietly while she was lost in wonder at the scene below. She felt cross with herself for having been caught off guard; still, she reflected, the little man might lead her to Polly.

"What have you done with my little brother?" she asked.

"Og," replied the green man. "Og; og!"

"You can't be Og!" said Penny crossly, in spite of her fear. "We left Og tied up back in the tunnel."

And he *wasn't* Og, she saw at once. This one had a sad kind of face with lines around the mouth as if he had been crying. The other Og (for she was now thinking of *both* men as "Og") had looked like a small imp – the kind that Pamela sometimes saw when she looked out of the window during Number Facts.

"*Og* og-og," cried the little man, still holding her tightly. As he spoke, two others a little bigger than he, and plumper, sprang out from behind a rock. One of them seized Penny, while the other gave the first man a hard shove.

The first man let go of Penny and began to whimper, whereupon both other men, who were each holding Penny with one arm, kicked him in the knee.

The sad little man sat down and began to cry.

"*Og! og! og!*" he said between his tears, pointing at Penny. He sounded, she thought, like Patsy when somebody took one of her toys away. "It's not *fair!*" Patsy would wail, in exactly the same tone. "I had it *first! It's mine!"

"I believe Pamela is right," Penny told herself. "They only have one word in their language and it's 'Og.' "

"*Og!*" said the man on her right – and it was an order, like "*March!*"

Penny looked around desperately for Yukon King, but there was no sign of him. Then she saw him, hidden behind some violet-coloured mushrooms at the edge of the tunnel, his small black nose just protruding a tiny bit.

"Poor Yukie," thought Penny as they dragged her away. "Here is his big chance to be a hero and he's muffed it again."

The two green men were pulling her toward some steps leading down the hill not far from the waterfall.

Penny was scared now – more for the others than for herself. How worried they would be when she didn't come back! What would Pamela do, she wondered; she wasn't a very good leader, though she was really quite smart. Penny wondered if she mightn't leave some trail they could follow but she could not move her hands to reach into her pockets. The little men walked on either side of her, holding her arms tight against her sides.

Out of the corner of her eye she detected a small movement behind another large clump of mushrooms. She looked again, and sure enough – it was Yukon King. The little dog was belly down on the ground, creeping from clump to clump and fairly quivering with excitement.

"Why, he's being a spy!" thought Penny with delight. "He's decided to find out where they're taking me and then go back and tell the others! What a clever dog he is after all." And she remembered a television show in which the giant malemute had trailed his master and brought help at the eleventh hour.

The climb down was a long and weary one. When they reached the bottom, Penny on looking up could no longer see any sign of a roof above them – only a greenish glow which looked like sky.

She saw that the country of the Ogs was bowl-shaped with pastel-coloured hills rising on every side, presumably to the roof of the great cavern beneath the earth. Halfway up one of these slopes, directly behind and above her, was the black mouth of the tunnel with the flashing cataract leaping from it in a graceful arc. She wondered what the others were thinking now back there in the dark, and what they were doing.

On the way down the two little men had stayed silent.

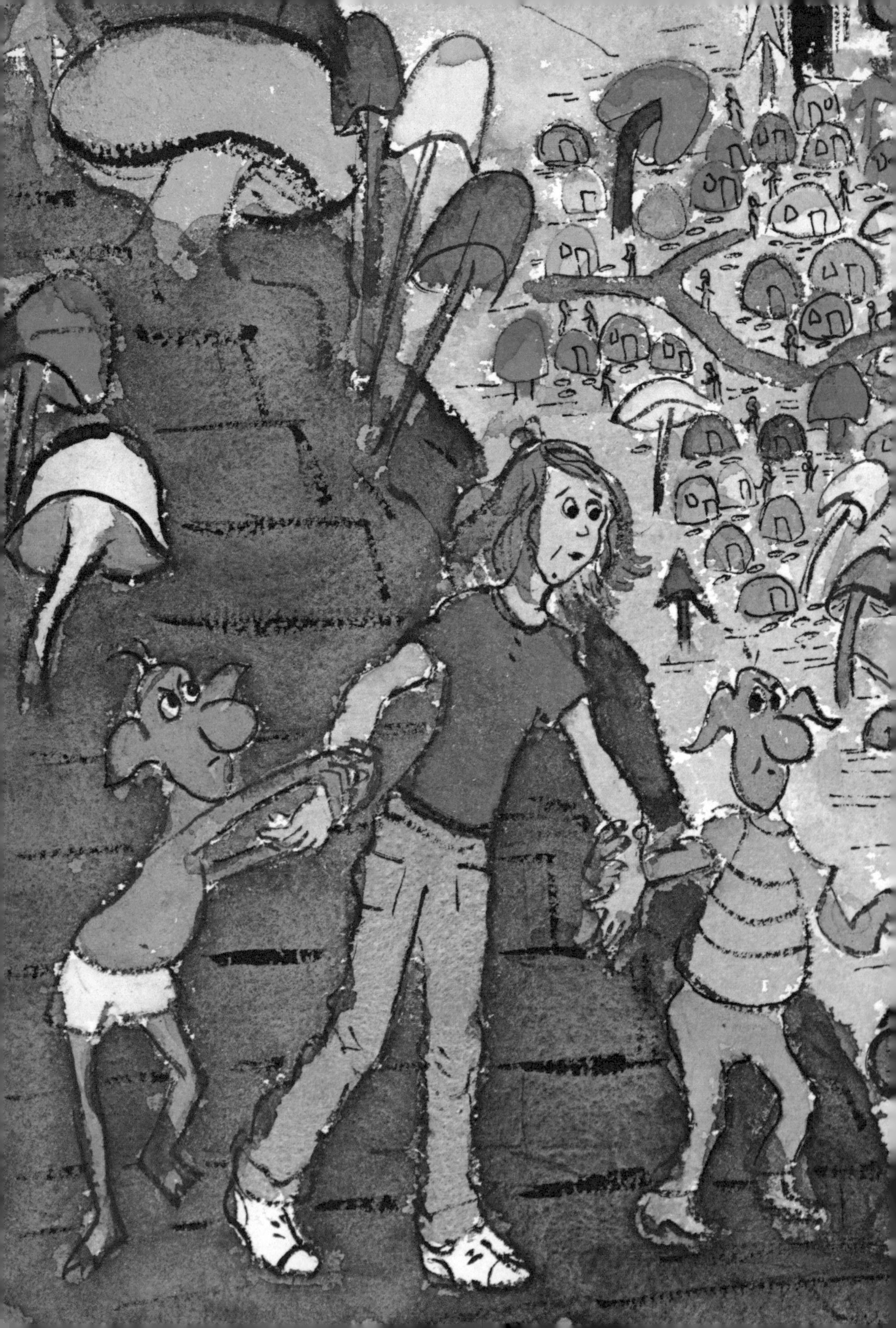

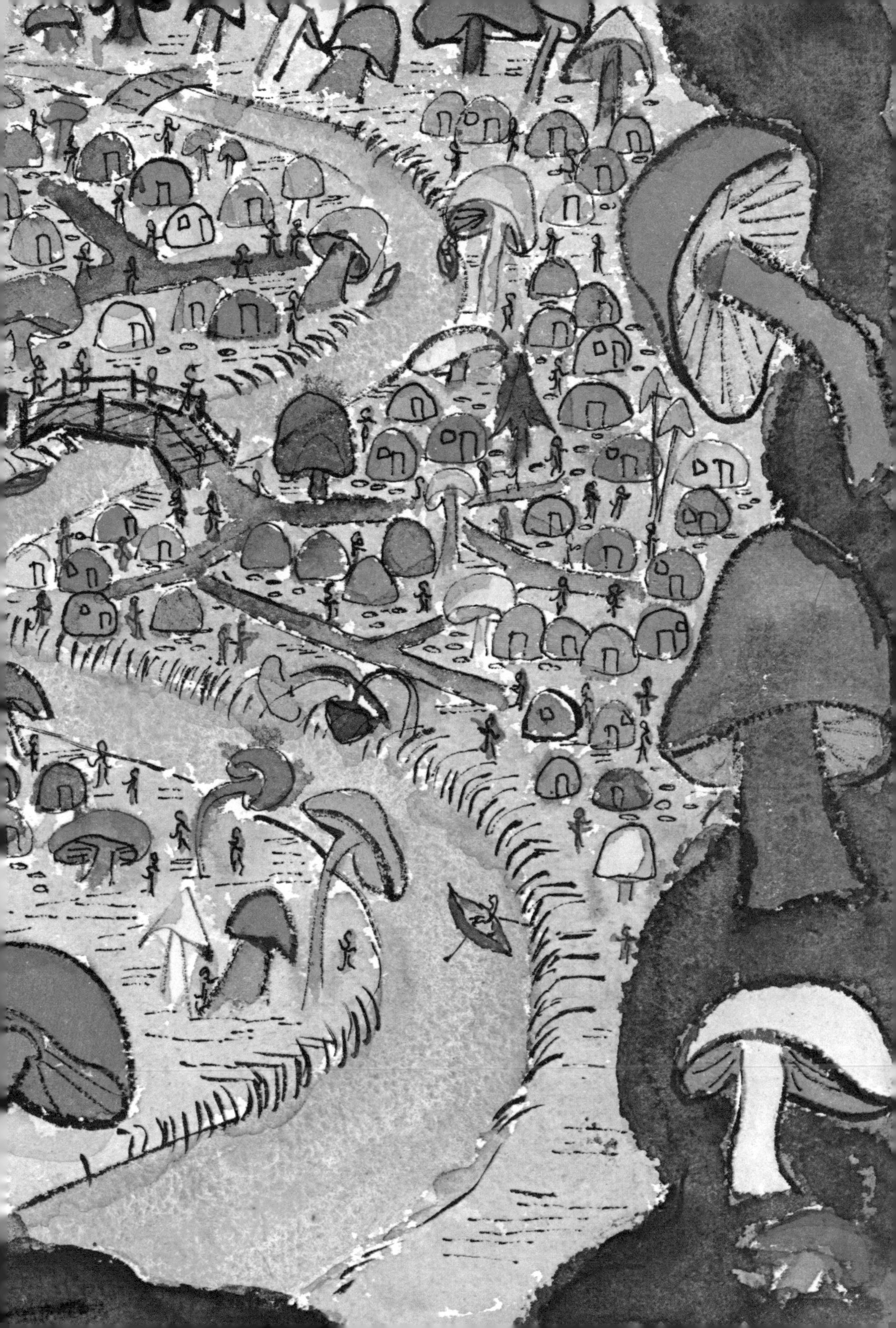

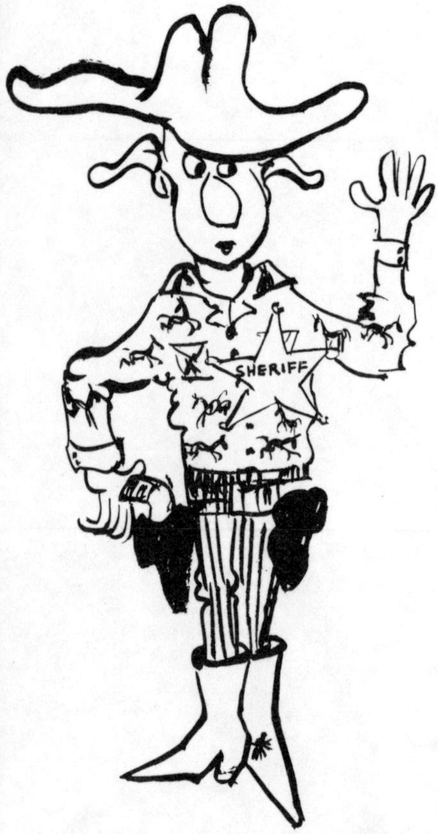
SHERIFF

Now, on the outskirts of the village of coloured mushroom houses, they met a group of several others. On seeing Penny, they all became very excited and each of the green men began to shout the one word "Og!" at the top of his voice, though with varying emphasis and inflection. They were all pointing at Penny and at the tunnel above them and getting absolutely nowhere as far as she could tell.

"It must be very hard to make yourself understood when there's only one word in the language," she told herself. "Still, it must make spelling ever so much easier." And in her mind she saw a schoolroom and a small green teacher with some small green pupils all solemnly writing the one word "Og" over and over again on the blackboard.

Now out of the group stepped a taller man. He raised his hand for silence and all the others stopped shouting "Og" and stepped back. To Penny's astonishment this creature was wearing a Western ten-gallon hat and a tin star pinned on his shirt. It was a very rusty tin star but she could just make out the word SHERIFF on it. The star looked familiar and Penny was pretty sure it was the one that Patsy had been given for Christmas, along with a Black Bart cowboy suit and a set of pearl-handled revolvers. Patsy had lost one of the guns and the star in the woods below the house. They had all searched for it in vain. Now here it was, pinned to the chest of a little man some two and a half feet high, with big staring eyes and floppy ears and solidly green from top to bottom.

"Og!" said the man with the sheriff's star in a booming voice of command. He pointed commandingly down the roadway which led in an easy curve along the base of the cliff down which they had just clambered. And the small procession moved off in that direction. The sheriff walked in front and then Penny, with her captors on either side, and then a sort of rabble of green people falling in behind all saying "Og!" to each other in whispers.

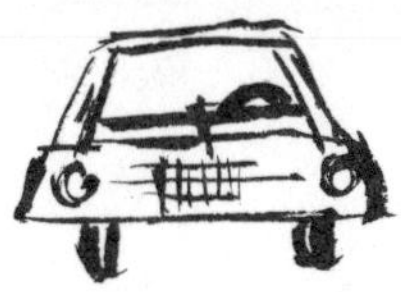

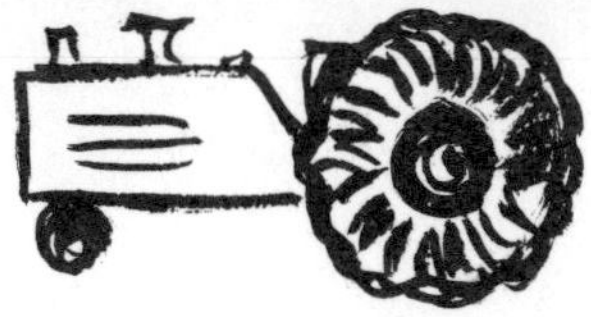

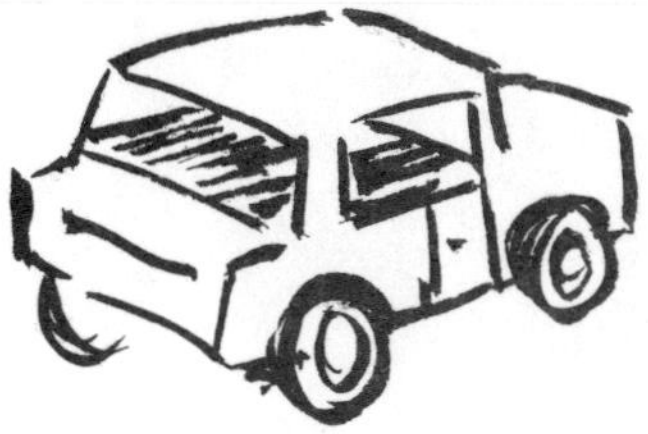

"This must be the main street," Penny said to herself as she walked along. And indeed it was quite apparent that many of the little dome-like buildings on either side were shops. They had stalls in front of them crammed with the strangest merchandise. Some of it seemed a little bit familiar.

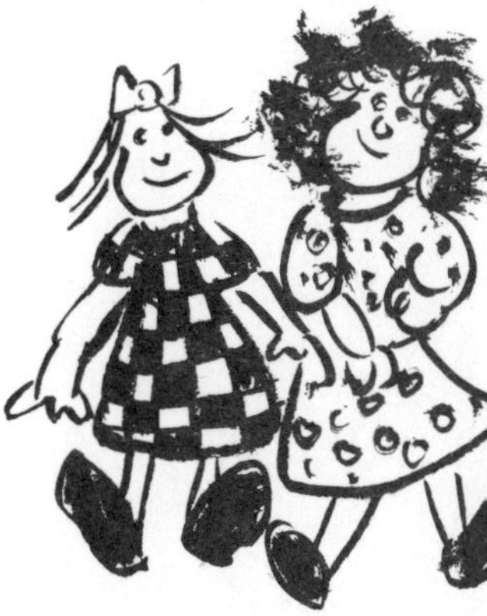

"Why, they're all like a lot of second-hand stores," she said, half aloud; and truth to tell they were: each of them filled with an amazing quantity of junk of every kind.

As the green men's legs were very short, they moved quite slowly down the street and Penny was able to look over quickly at several of the open stalls. In one of them she saw three toy cars and a toy tractor, all rusty, which she was sure had once belonged to Peter. (He was always leaving them out in the rain and losing them.) In another she saw a pile of comic books including several *Mad Monsters* that Pam had accused Patsy of throwing away. A third stall was full of dolls, including a Panda bear that Patsy and the twins had dropped in the frog pond, and several other faded dolls. Then Penny broke into a shrill scream: there at the front of the stall was her very own doll Elizabeth Anne, with the hair that really combed! Penny's heart leaped. So that's where poor Elizabeth Anne had got to. Now, she told herself firmly, she would never *never* go back above ground without taking Elizabeth Anne with her. She fixed the little stall securely in her mind so that she would remember it later.

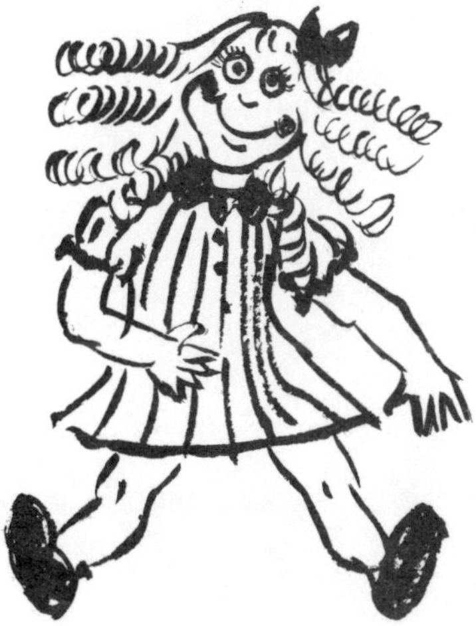

There were several more stalls: a dress shop containing some old Dress-Up clothes that had gone missing weeks before. And another stall full of broken and discarded toys. And then what was quite obviously a butcher shop, with stalls full of small rabbits, some already dressed and hanging by their feet and some alive and hopping about in cages. There was something odd about those rabbits, Penny thought. She looked more closely as she went by: there, in

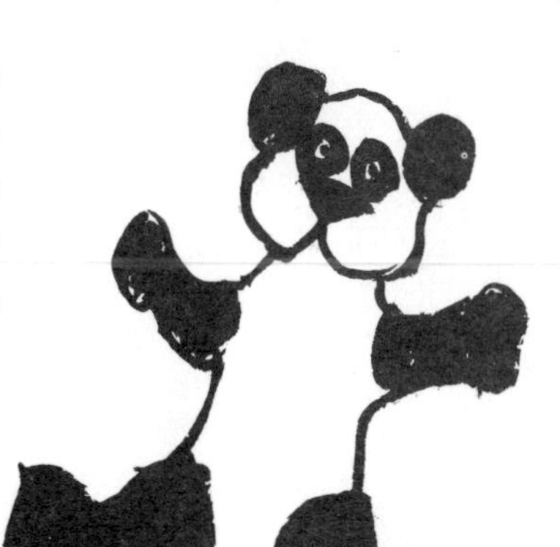

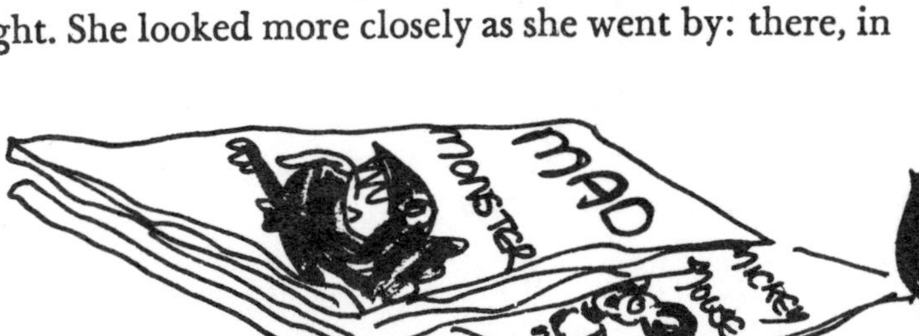
MAD
MONSTER
Mickey Mouse

the middle, with what was quite obviously a price tag around his neck, was Earless Osdick himself!

"Why, I believe the silly little men think he's some kind of rabbit," Penny thought. Osdick saw her and jumped up and let out what he thought was a bark and Penny's heart almost broke at the sight of him, sitting in that wire cage like so much meat, with a price tag on him. Something had to be done, she realized, and done quickly – or he'd be sold and eaten. (*And the Pollywog!* she thought, *do they think he is a rabbit too?*)

But there was little she could do. She was surrounded by a swarm of people – men, women and even some tiny green children – all looking at her and pointing and chattering among themselves.

They had by this time reached the end of the street and now came to a cave cut into the hillside. Here everybody stopped. The "sheriff" motioned to Penny's captors to bring her forward, and they did so – not roughly, for they had never been the least bit rough, but firmly. They went into the cave and Penny saw that it was divided up into rooms, each room with a set of crude wooden bars in front of it. All these rooms – cells, really – were empty except one. And there, to Penny's great relief and joy, peering out from behind the bars, was the Pollywog himself.

As usual he was in jail, and plotting to escape.

6/Peter Adopts a Disguise

Back in the tunnel, Pamela, Patsy and Peter waited . . . and waited . . . and waited. Pamela had watched Penny's thin form, silhouetted against the light at the end of the tunnel; she had seen it stop, climb over something, move on and disappear. She tried to show that she wasn't worried for she did not want to scare the little ones. But she was growing desperately uneasy.

"C'mon!" said Patsy, "let's get moving!"

"I'm hungry," Peter announced.

Pamela remembered the little jars and boxes of candies she had taken from the cupboards. When she pulled them from her pockets they were a bit gooey from having been in the water, but they were better than nothing. She divided them up carefully, saving two portions for Penny and the Pollywog. The three children began to stuff the sweet sticky mass into their mouths. Then Peter remembered their prisoner.

"Here, Og," he said, amiably, "you can have one of mine."

The green man was still lying on his stomach and trying without success to wriggle out of his bonds. He took the small candy that Peter put in his mouth and licked at it gratefully.

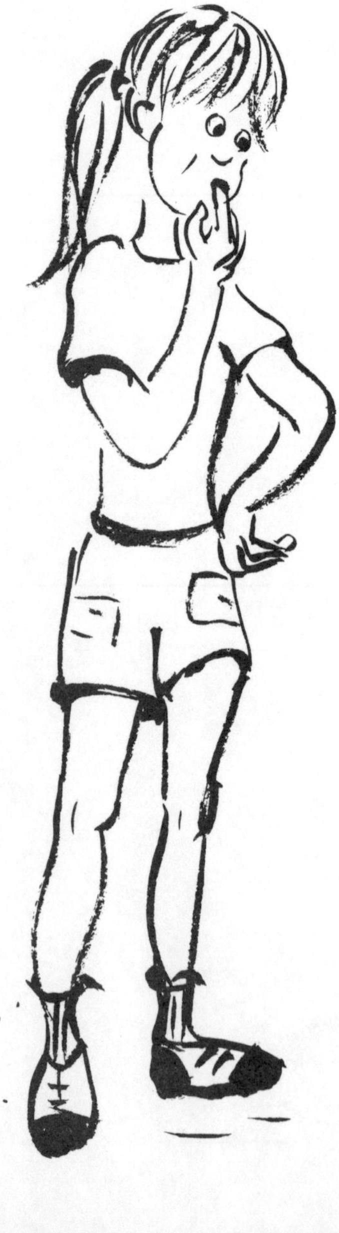

"C'mon, let's get moving!" Patsy said again.

"No," Pamela said firmly. "Penny told us to stay here."

She was really very worried now and this was a new sensation for Pamela who seldom worried about anything. But then she had never been in charge of anything before. It had always been Penny and now Penny was gone. Pamela felt her brows knit up into a little frown. She had seen just such a frown on Penny's face many a time, and often she had wondered why Penny frowned like that. Now she knew. It's really not much fun being the boss, Pamela thought to herself. She realized that pretty soon she would have to make some sort of decision. Penny had been gone for some time and Pamela was certain that something sinister had happened to her. She and the two younger children could not stay here, on a narrow ledge in a dark tunnel and in wet clothes, for much longer.

"C'mon," Patsy chirped for the third time. "Let's get cracking!" It was a phrase she had heard her father use more than once. She did not quite know what it meant but it sounded suitably active.

It was Patsy, not Peter, who was going to be the problem, Pamela realized. The little boy, quite unconcerned, was lying on his stomach next to Og, and pushing his boat around in the water.

"B-r-r-r-r-r!" he said to himself. "In my motorboat. Crossing the Atlantic Ocean."

"I think maybe we had all better move up toward the light," Pamela said at last.

"What about him?" said Peter, pointing to Og.

Pamela realized, with a sigh, that she must make another decision.

"Well," she said at last, "we'll just have to leave him here. Now come on, stay close together and don't make any noise."

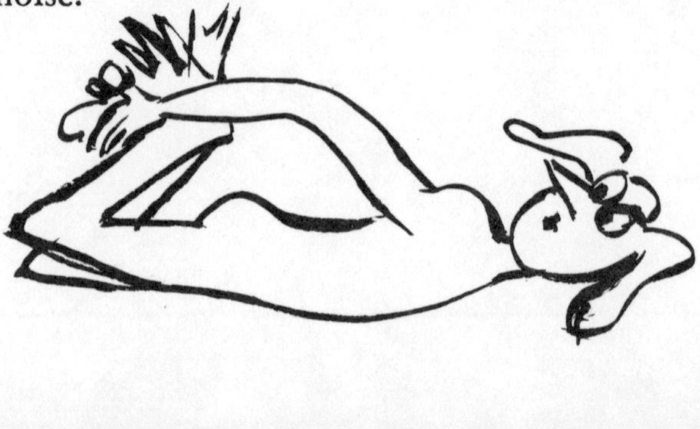

"Og!" said Og in a plaintive way.

"Here," said Peter generously. "You can play with my boat while we're gone." And he set it down about an inch from Og's nose. As they left, Peter looked back and saw that the sharp-nosed Og was staring fixedly at the boat as if hypnotized. His eyes, Peter noted, were crossed like Patsy's. Peter wished he could cross his eyes like that.

The three children moved silently along the damp ledge, stopping every few minutes to listen. How angry Penny would be, thought Pamela, if it turned out that she was perfectly all right after all! Maybe they were gumming up some secret plan by disobeying orders. After all, Penny had been very firm about the three of them staying put until she returned. Oh dear, thought Pamela, it's very difficult making decisions.

"I hear a little splash," Patsy whispered.

It was true. There was a sloshing sound just ahead. The children stopped and huddled close to the wall, not knowing quite what to do.

Something soft touched Pamela's hand and she jumped in fright. She was about to scream but then remembered that she couldn't because she was the leader.

"It's Yukie," said Peter. "He went with Penny. I saw him."

Pamela had been so busy thinking and planning that she had forgotten about the little dog. Now she recognized him with relief.

"Yukie! Where's Penny?"

The dog growled softly and turned his head toward the tunnel, looked back at Pamela for a moment and then started to move toward the light at the end.

"Something *has* happened," Pamela said. "He's trying to lead us."

"I *told* you he'd pertect us," Peter said.

73

The three children followed the dog, climbing over the net and noting, with curiosity, the little boats still moored in the channel.

At the edge of the tunnel, Yukon King stopped. The three children stopped behind him. Then the dog squeezed quietly around the big rock at the entrance and turned his head as a signal for the children to follow. They did so and found themselves under an enormous clump of giant pink mushrooms.

Yukon King poked his black nose out between two of the great stalks and looked around. Pamela peered out with him and saw, unfolded before her, the same vista that had awed Penny: the great waterfall, the river winding off into the distance, the copses of brightly coloured mushrooms, the bridges and the road, the strange bright houses and the green people, tiny dots below, moving about in the soft glow.

Yukon King gave a low growl and Pamela saw two green men climbing up the steps beside the waterfall, directly below her. She motioned the others to lie flat and keep quiet. The two little men passed within a foot or so of the mushroom patch. Pamela noticed to her surprise that they were both wearing Davy Crockett coonskin caps. Peter and Patsy had once owned a couple just like them when the craze was at its height.

The two little men disappeared into the tunnel.

"We've got to move," Pamela whispered. "They'll find Og back there and he'll tell them we're out here. Hurry!"

"He can't tell them much," said Patsy. "All he can say is 'Og!' *Og! Og! Og!* That's all he can say."

As she spoke Yukon King was wriggling flat on his belly toward the next copse of mushrooms. He looked over his shoulder at Pamela and she beckoned the others to follow.

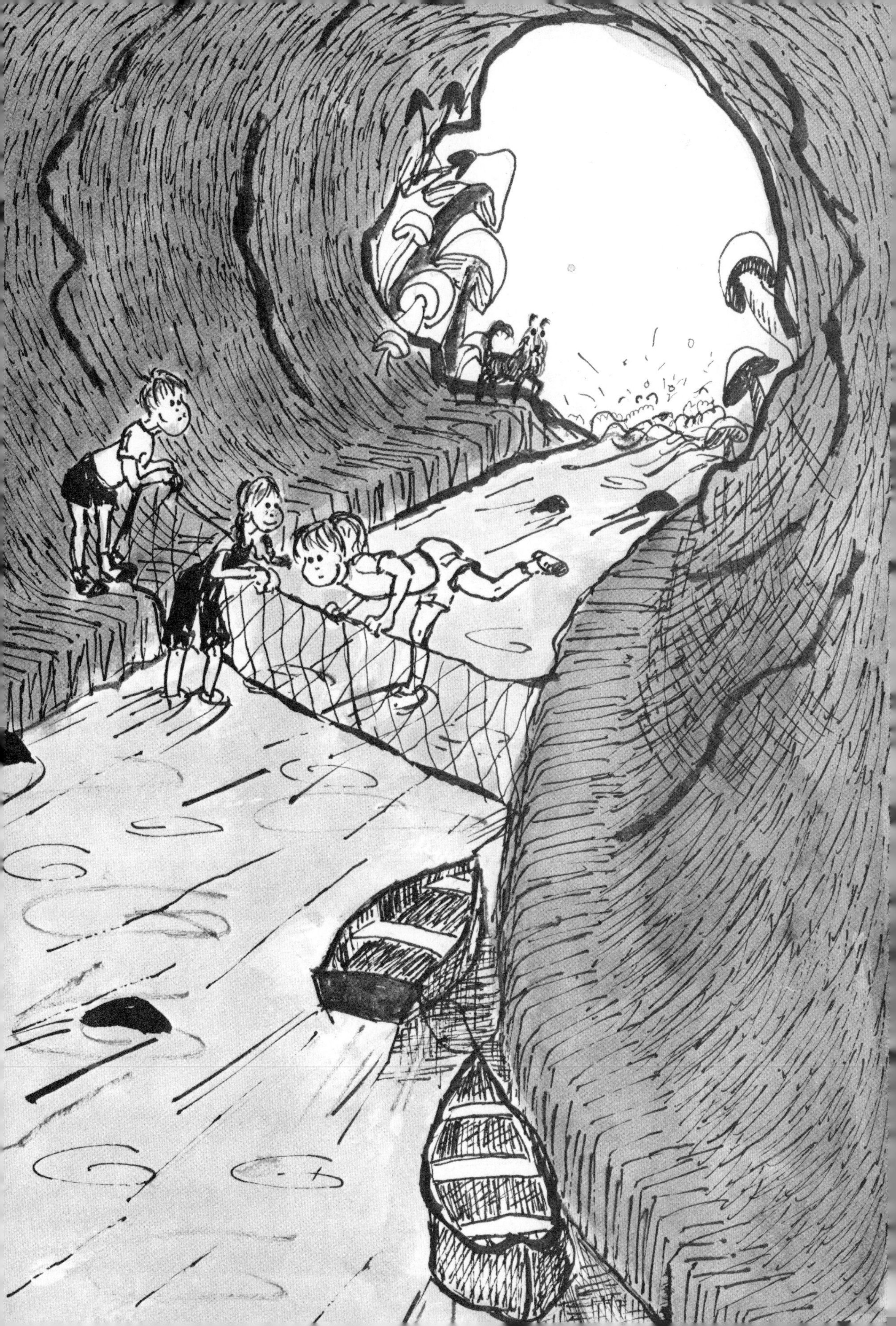

"It's just like being Indians!" Patsy whispered in delight as they crawled after him.

The little dog was leading them along the edge of a sort of ridge that seemed to dominate the village of round huts below. They moved, in this fashion, for several hundred yards, from copse to copse, until they reached a spot just overlooking the edge of the settlement. Yukon King growled again and pointed downward with his nose, as he had seen bird dogs do in Father's copy of *True Lies*, the man's magazine.

Pamela looked below and saw a cave tucked away in the edge of the hillside, at the point where it curved around behind the settlement.

"I believe he's trying to tell us that Penny is down there," she said.

"Well, c'mon!" said Patsy, "let's go!"

But Pamela was not to be hurried. She was looking the situation over carefully and trying to decide on the best course of action. Supposing the green people had captured Penny and the Pollywog, as seemed likely. Then Pamela and the others must at all costs avoid being captured. But how could they stay out of the green men's clutches and at the same time free the prisoners – if they *were* prisoners? Certainly not by plunging ahead without some sort of plan.

In the first place, the slope below them was bare of any cover. Anybody going down that way would be spotted at once. In the last *Mad Monster* story, Pamela remembered, Garth Greatheart had disguised himself as a Red Martian and moved freely among the enemy. But then Garth Greatheart had unlimited access to expensive costumes. (He was always changing his shirt in alleyways, and putting on that ridiculous blue cloak, and hypnotizing people by wiggling his fingers.) Pamela had a feeling that if Garth

Greatheart was on the spot now he would make a mess of things.

"Penny's in that cave down there," Pamela said to the others. "I'm sure of it, from the way Yukie is growling and pointing. They've probably got her locked up."

"Then we'll just go down and get her out," said Patsy.

"It's not that easy, they'd spot us sure. They're green, you know, and we're white."

"Well," said Patsy, "we could be green, too." And she pulled the tube of green paint out of her pocket. "I was going to use it to paint some of my frogs, but you can have it," she said. "The frogs are pretty green anyway."

Pamela took the paint and thought a moment.

"It won't work," she said at last, shaking her head. "We're much too big. They'd still spot us."

"Pam," said Peter, tugging at her shorts. "Let me go. I'm little."

"He is, too," said Patsy. "He's *really* little."

It was true. Peter was the exact height of the green people – though much stockier, Pamela realized.

"All right," she said, making up her mind suddenly. "We can't just sit here and do nothing. Pete – you're going to be a spy. We'll colour you green and you go down below. Try to find Penny and see if she knows where Polly is. Tell her where we are and then report back."

"And don't forget Earless Osdick," said Patsy.

"Oh, dear," said Pamela, "I forgot about him. That makes one more."

She realized, with something close to panic, that the tight little group which had started out was slowly becoming separated: Osdick, Paul, Penny – and now Peter. She didn't like the idea of this; on the other hand, she couldn't see any better plan than the one they had adopted. Pamela felt about five years older than she had when they started

down the tunnel from the Playhouse. She wished that it was she, not Peter, who was going down below, but she knew this to be impossible. She was too big.

"Let's get the paint on Peter," she said. Peter took off his T-shirt. She and Patsy began to squeeze gobs of the paint out on their hands and rub it into Peter's body. They coloured his tummy and chest and his back and his arms green. His shorts were green already but his legs and his face and even his hair had to be made quite green.

When all the paint had been used, Pamela stepped back and had a look at him.

"Well," she said slowly. "You might just get away with it, Pete. Though you're awfully sticky!"

Peter felt quite pleased. Like all red-blooded boys he had always wanted to paint himself green, but being a good child he had fought the desire. Now, at last, he had achieved a small ambition.

"Try not to be too long," Pamela whispered. "We'll wait right here. Okay?"

"Sure," said Peter. He stepped out of the mushroom copse and started down the slope. Then he came back.

"I forgot my tractor," he said.

"Oh, Peter! At a time like this."

He grabbed around in the sand, found it, and then began to clamber easily down the long slopes, picking his way between the big boulders and through the clumps of brightly coloured mushrooms, until he reached the roadway below.

Because of the steepness of the cliff he did not go directly downward but moved at an angle back toward the river. Thus when he reached the base of the hill he was no longer directly below the children's hiding place but quite close to the flight of steps down which Penny had been led by her captors.

He stopped in the shade of a great clump of scarlet mushrooms. The soft light filtered down through them, glowing redly on his green features and giving him the dark look of a small copper-coloured Indian. Peter looked about him carefully, got his bearings and then stepped boldly from the shadows.

WHAM! He collided headlong with a small scurrying green figure also coming down from the hill and the two of them staggered back at the force of the blow.

Peter was the first to recover his breath. And as he did so he looked straight into the impish and angry features of Og, the man whom not half an hour ago they had left neatly trussed up inside the tunnel.

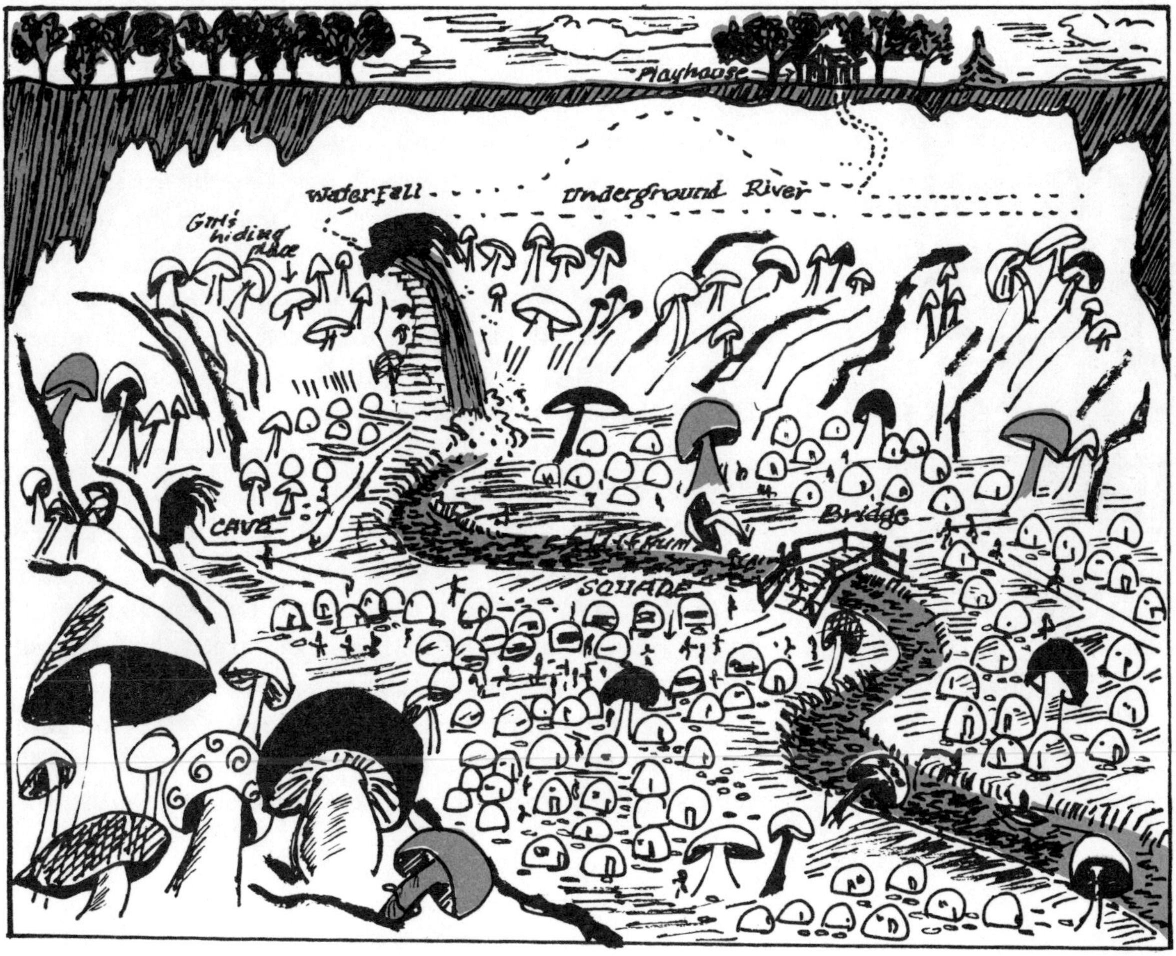
Playhouse
Waterfall
Underground River
Girl's hiding place
CAVE
Bridge
SQUARE

7/How Penny Broke Jail

When Penny saw the Pollywog gripping the bars of his cell and staring out at her, she almost cried with joy. The Pollywog, in his turn, began to jump up and down, crowing with delight.

The green man with the sheriff's badge put a very large key into a very large and rusty lock, swung open the barred door and motioned to Penny to go in. She did so and in a moment was hugging the Pollywog. She heard the door clang behind her and only then realized that she, too, was locked securely in a jail cell.

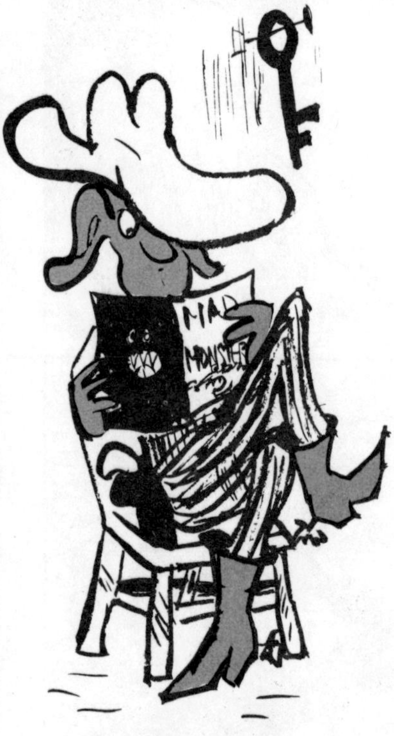
MAD
MONSTER

The green sheriff hung the key on a nail in the wall. Then he put his hat down low over his nose, slumped down in a chair, picked a comic book from a pile that lay beside it, and settled down to read.

Penny put the Pollywog down and peeped out through the bars to try to find exactly what he was reading.

"Why," she said, "it's a *Wyatt Earp* comic–and there's a *Mad Monster* at the top of the pile."

Now Penny began to think of all the familiar things that she had seen in the stalls and the green man dressed like a pretend-sheriff and the comic books in the pile.

"They must come up through holes in the ground and steal things that people up above leave lying around!" Penny said to herself. The more she thought about it, the more it made sense. She had noticed more than once that if you left something lying around it was liable to disappear forever. Father, for instance, was always complaining that somebody had stolen one of his tools and she could still hear her mother saying, "Now, now, dear, it couldn't have got up and *walked* away. If you just didn't leave your things lying around you wouldn't misplace them." Penny thought of the tiny saw which had made such a neat trap door in the floor of the Playhouse and she made a mental note to be more careful of her own things in the future.

"Og!" said the Pollywog suddenly.

The sheriff looked up from his reading.

"Og," he said absently, and turned a page.

"Og-og *og*!" the Pollywog chattered back at him.

"Why, Polly!" exclaimed Penny, "you clever little boy! You've actually learned the language."

"Og, Og," said the Pollywog smugly.

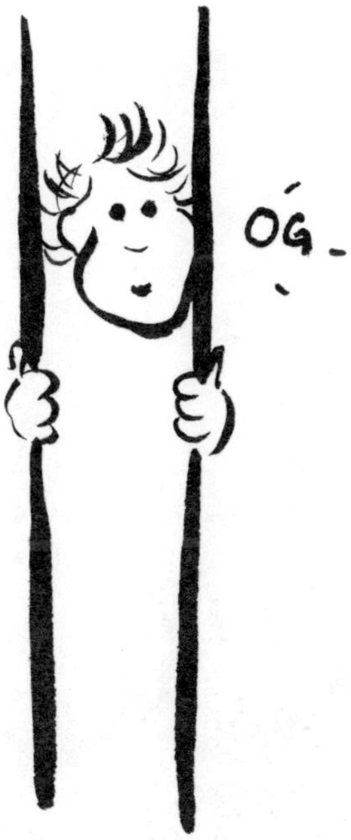
OG

But then it occurred to Penny that the Pollywog had *always* known the language. The only word he ever said *was* "Og." In fact, she had noticed him using it to other babies who occasionally visited their home. The two babies would stare at each other for minutes on end, occasionally poking each other in the eye with a rattle and passing the time of day by saying "Og," over and over again.

"How useful you are, Polly!" Penny said. "You can be my interpreter. Ask the sheriff what he intends to do with us."

"Og?" shouted the Pollywog through the bars.

"Og-og!" said the sheriff, not looking up.

"Og-og!" said the Pollywog, brightly, to Penny.

Penny shook her head sadly. The trouble was, she realized, that while the Pollywog could talk Og language, he couldn't talk *hers*. Once again she felt herself very close to tears. Nothing was going right. She and the Pollywog were in jail. Earless Osdick was going to be eaten. Goodness knows what had happened to the others.

"Oh, Polly," she said, "we *are* in a mess!"

"One heck of a mess!" muttered a voice. Penny jerked her head around. She could have sworn it came from the direction of the sheriff, but he seemed absorbed in his cowboy comic.

"He can't understand much of it," thought Penny. But then she noticed a strange thing. As the sheriff peered at each comic page, his lips moved slowly, like a small child learning to read.

Penny watched him for a moment in amazement. Then she spoke:

"Excuse me!" she said, in a challenging voice.

The sheriff slowly put his book down and turned to her.

"You speakin' to me, pardner?" he said, in a slow drawl.

"Why, he talks cowboy talk!" Penny exclaimed in delight. "I bet he learns it from the comic books!"

Then falling quickly into the lingo, she said:

"What do you figger on doing with us, sheriff?"

"Don't rightly know," said the sheriff. "Never had no one in jail afore this. String you up, mos' likely."

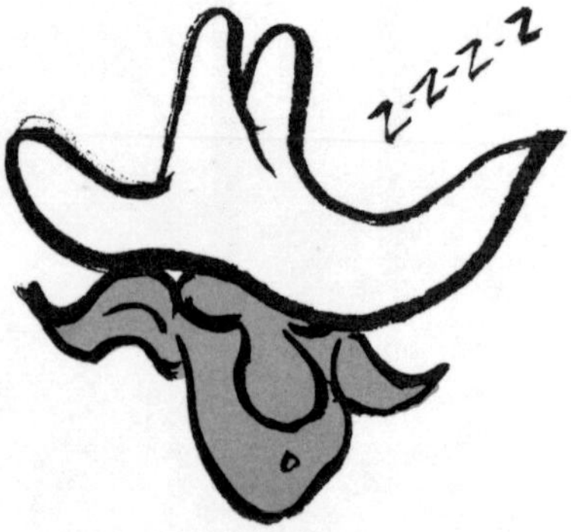
Z-Z-Z-Z-Z

Penny shivered at the thought. But her curiosity got the better of her fear.

"Why don't you speak like this *all* the time?" she asked him. "Why do you always speak in – in *ogs*?"

"It's easier," said the sheriff, shining his star on his sleeve. "Don't take no brain work." He yawned deeply, and went back to reading his *Wyatt Earp* comic and Penny could get no more out of him. A few minutes later, he dropped his comic book listlessly and drifted off into a deep slumber.

"He snores just like Father," Penny told herself.

Hanging suspended just above him she could see the

great key to the cell door dangling. She had read of many situations when Good Guys, held in jail, had sneaked a key away from a sleeping sheriff, let themselves out and gone off in pursuit of Bad Guys. Indeed such a situation had occurred in *Lucy Lawless, Girl Rustler*. Lucy had made a lasso out of her two stockings, thrown it over the key and escaped while the sheriff was still snoring in the jailhouse.

Penny thought about that for a while but realized that she could not duplicate the feat. She wasn't very good with a lasso, and besides she wasn't wearing any stockings.

It occurred to her that a long stick might do the trick, but the cell was quite bare. There was nothing in it that she could use at all. In fact, she realized with a shock, there was no one else in the cell – not even the Pollywog!

"Polly!" Penny called, "where are you?"

She heard a little bark and, turning about, saw him. He was outside the cell, on all fours as usual, crawling about in delight at being free.

"Oh, Polly!" cried Penny, "you've escaped again! However do you do it?"

But the Pollywog did not tell. For one thing he couldn't talk: for another, it was a secret. Does Mandrake the Magician tell all he knows? Certainly not. Years later, when the Pollywog tried to remember how he always escaped, he couldn't. By then his mind was too crowded with other things, such as how to work out the square root of 925 and whether or not an agate was a good trade for three smokies.

"Polly!" Penny whispered. "The key. Get me the key!" And she pointed toward the wall above the sheriff.

The Pollywog headed across the floor at a great rate, straight for the sleeping man.

"Oh, the clever little thing!" said Penny. "He knows exactly what to do."

But the Pollywog was not interested in the key. It was

the pile of comic books on which his beady little eyes were fastened. For most of his life he had wanted to be alone with a pile of comic books. Often he had stared out from behind the bars of his crib or playpen and watched wistfully while the other children lay on their stomachs on the floor and read *Batman, Superman, Heckle and Jeckell* and others. But the Pollywog was never allowed to have any. Instead he was given horrible little books made out of cloth, with foolish pictures of balls and blocks and kittens on each page. Nobody ever *did* anything in these books. There were no pictures of funny men hitting other funny men and going WHAM! or ZOWIE! Only pictures of Balls with big B's under them and Cows with big C's. Worst of all, from the Pollywog's point of view, these little books were so strongly constructed that it was quite impossible to tear them into bits.

The Pollywog almost dived into the sheriff's pile of comics. He seized a *Mad Monster* and began turning the pages avidly. He could not read a word, but the pictures were very exciting. There was an especially large dog with green eyes and huge nostrils that the Pollywog liked enormously. This was not actually a dog; it was the Mad Monster himself, but the Pollywog didn't know that. He thought that everything that walked on four feet was a dog. He barked at the picture of the Mad Monster and waited for it to bark back, but nothing happened. So he tore the page out and crawled over to the cell and gave it to Penny to look at.

Penny was in an agony of frustration. Here they were so near to freedom and all that little Pollywog thought of was comic books!

"Look, Polly," she said, very carefully and slowly. "You've got to get me that key. See? The key. Up there." And she pointed.

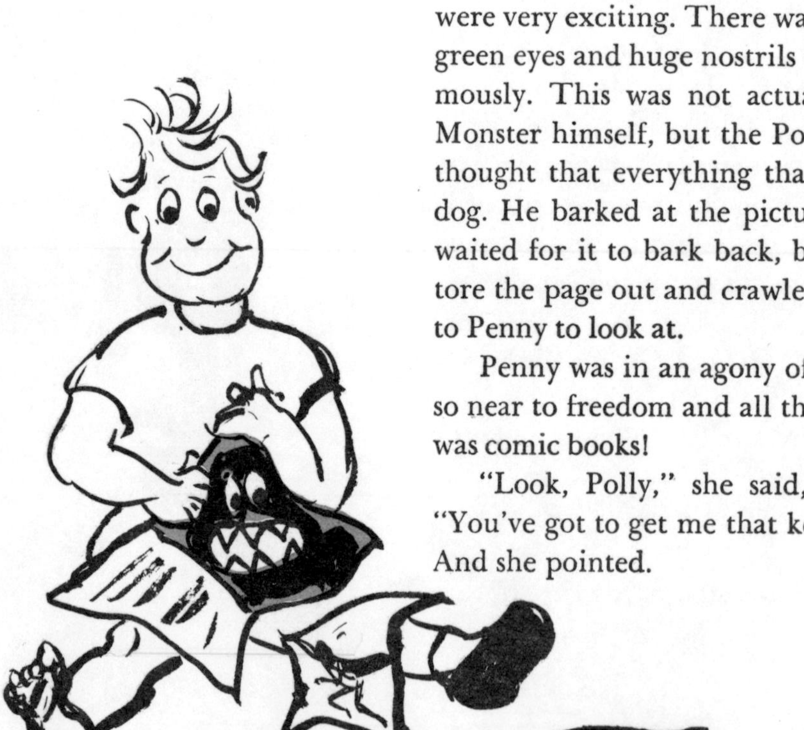

The Pollywog crawled back at high speed and seized another comic book.

Penny watched him helplessly. What on earth could she do? In a few minutes the sheriff would wake up or somebody would come and then they would be no better off than before.

An idea came to her.

"Paul!" she said, in a sharp, commanding voice. "Don't you dare touch that key. Leave it alone now!"

The Pollywog dropped his copy of *Larry the Ghoul* and looked up with sudden interest.

"You leave that key alone now, Paul!" Penny said, again trying her best to sound like her mother.

Paul looked up at the key and his face took on the same look of cunning that it did when his mother told him he mustn't go near the jelly beans.

The key was too high for him to reach but this did not faze him. He hauled himself up on the little stool beside the sheriff, stretched up his hand and pulled the key down.

"Can I have a comic book, please Polly?" Penny asked him. She was far too knowing to ask for the key.

The Pollywog rolled off the stool and onto the pile of scattered comics. He tore another page out of the *Mad Monster* and took it over to Penny. She had no time to be gentle. She seized the baby by his arm, and forced the key out of his fist. It was tough going for he held onto it very firmly. She was glad it was just a key and not an all-day sucker, otherwise she knew she'd never have got it away from him. For, as everybody knows, the hardest thing in the world is to take candy from a baby.

The Pollywog was outraged. Penny could see by the outthrust of his lower lip that he was about to cry. She knew she must move quickly and she did. She reached through the bars, slid the key into the lock, turned it and

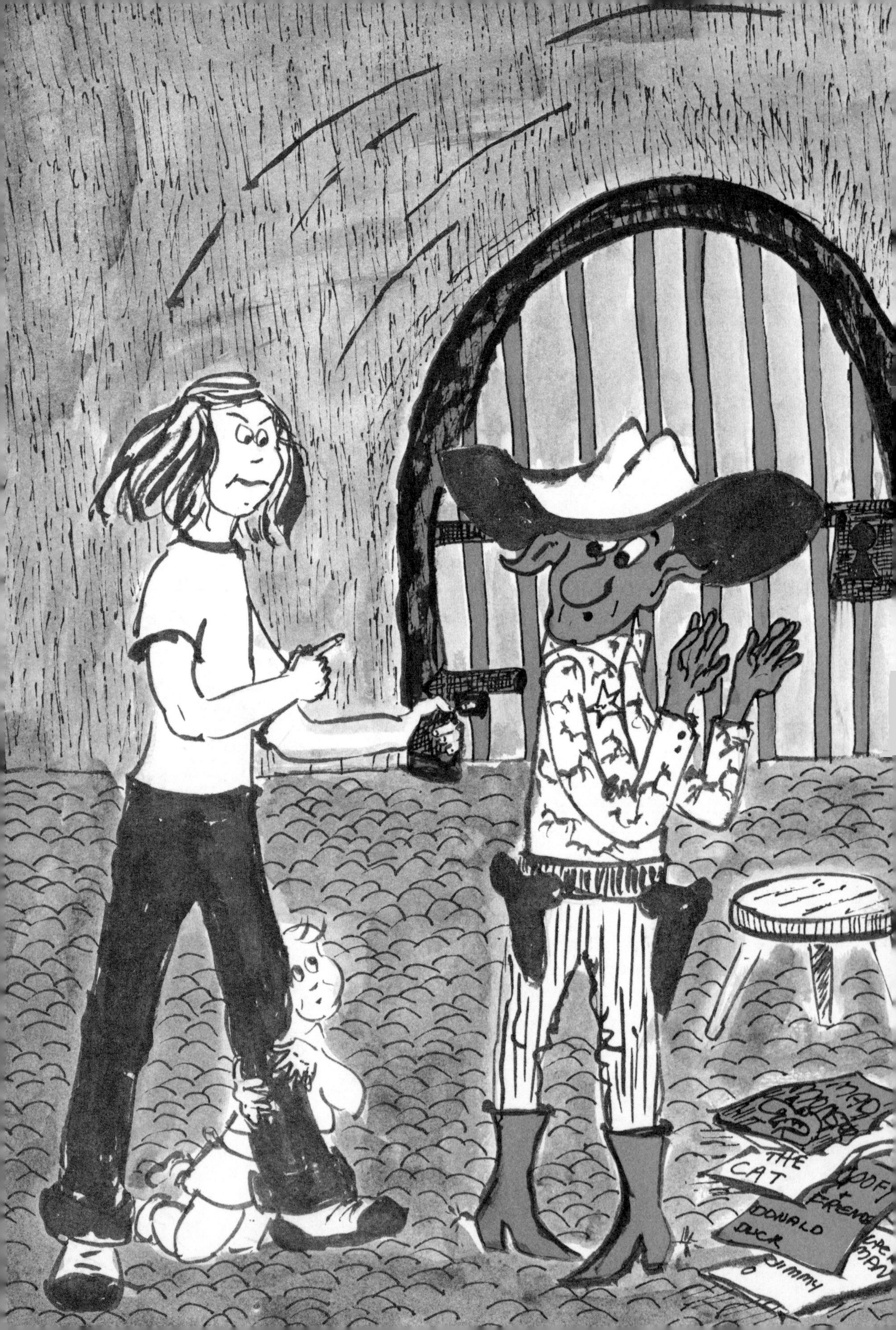
MAD
THE CAT
DONALD DUCK
JIMMY

flung open the cell door.

The Pollywog was so surprised by this that he forgot to cry. Penny reached down and kissed him, so he would know they were still friends. Then, keeping him close to her, she began to slide along the far wall past the sleeping sheriff.

A thought occurred to her: if the sheriff awoke they would be at his mercy. There was only one thing to do. She must take his guns away from him at once!

She tiptoed over, reached down, and pulled both guns from their holsters. As she did so she noticed that one was a cap gun and the other a water pistol.

"Why," she told herself, "these people are just like little children, playing at being cowboys."

Suddenly the sheriff awoke and stood up as if shot. Penny knew exactly what to do. She shoved one of the guns in his back.

"Put 'em up!" she said. "I got you covered."

The sheriff's hands shot to the sky.

"Yuh got the drop on me, pardner," he said, admiration in his voice.

"One false move and you're dead!" Penny said, grateful that she had read *Lucy Lawless, Girl Rustler*.

"March!" she said, pointing at the cell, but the sheriff refused to move.

"It's my bounden duty to defend my sacred office with my life," he said. It sounded as if he'd memorized it.

Penny didn't know quite what to do. Then she noticed the sheriff's hands were trembling.

"Think of your wife and children!" she said.

"Yer right, man," said the sheriff, much relieved, and allowed himself to be herded into the cell.

Only when he was securely locked up did he look confused. "But I've *got* no wife and children," he complained.

"Too bad," said Penny, locking the cell securely. And then, because she had a kind heart, she went over to the pile of comic books, selected several and gave them to the green sheriff.

"Thank yuh, ma'am," he said. "That's right neighbourly of yuh. You're a real gentleman – for a rustler!"

"All right, Polly," Penny whispered. (She always seemed to be whispering, she thought to herself.) "Let's get out of here."

She tucked him securely under her arm and started for the entrance to the cave, sliding along the wall and keeping in the shadows as she had seen the Good Guys do on TV. If somebody else entered, Penny meant to surprise him.

And sure enough – somebody else *did* enter: another green man with weirdly mottled features and shiny white teeth. To her horror, Penny saw that he was carrying Earless Osdick by the neck. Indeed, the little cat seemed near strangulation.

Penny knew what she had to do. She stepped out of the shadows, behind the green man, and shoved her gun in his back.

"Reach, pardner!" she said, in a deep voice. "I've got yuh covered. One move and you're a dead hombre."

She tried to put as much force into her words as possible but, to her dismay, they had no effect at all.

"That doesn't fool me," she heard the green man say. "It's a toy gun and it won't even work. Put it down!"

And as he spoke, he turned fiercely toward her, his fists clenched and his eyes menacing.

Penny dropped the gun with a clatter and shrank back against the wall.

8/Killer Kane, Scourge of the Underworld

When Peter recognized Og, after bumping into him at the foot of the cliff, his immediate reaction was to ask for his boat back. Og, he noticed, was holding it in one hand and Peter figured it was *his* turn to play with it now.

Then he remembered he was supposed to be disguised and his next thought was to run away as swiftly as he could. Og was giving him a menacing look and Peter wasn't at all sure that he wasn't recognized under the green paint. After all his ears weren't nearly as big and floppy as those of the real green people.

But after a moment's hesitation he stood his ground. If he ran away now, he realized, it would only make the other more suspicious.

"Og!" said Og, angrily.

To which Peter replied "Og" in as apologetic a manner as he could.

He went over and began to dust Og's trousers off, then he stopped when he saw that some of the green paint was coming off his hands.

"Og," said Peter again in an amiable voice.

Og looked at him a little suspiciously, as if trying to place him from somewhere. Then – for he was apparently in a great hurry – he scuttled away along the river bank.

Peter turned in the opposite direction, heading for the cave under the hill where Yukon King had indicated Penny was being held.

He seemed to be on some sort of main street for he now found himself in the middle of a crowd of green people, all scurrying about and apparently shopping at stalls that lined both sides of the roadway.

It was a very curious sensation for Peter to move about with people who were all his size. Mostly he was used to throwing his head back to look up into the faces of the adults he talked to. Now he felt like an adult himself and it gave him a good deal of confidence.

Nobody paid much attention to him. The green people all seemed to be in a great hurry. They darted from stall to stall, pricing the things for sale, and then they darted along the street clutching their purchases and looking constantly at their wrist watches. Peter noted that the wrist watches were all toy wrist watches of the kind that he got in his stocking at Christmas (and usually lost). Why, he thought, they really don't know what time it is at all!

They wore a very strange assortment of clothes, he noticed. Some wore brightly coloured clothes made of some odd velvety material but many were wearing what appeared to be dolls' clothes and some seemed to be wearing Dress-Up clothes. They pushed their tiny green babies about in small carts — toy wagons or dolls' baby carriages, usually rusty ones. And they wore hats of every description: old straw hats, battered derbies, children's tams — anything and everything.

Peter had gone only a few steps when he noticed a pile of toy cars in one of the little stalls.

"Why, there's my little dump truck," he said to himself. "The one I lost down in the woods."

He stopped and peered at the stall. He felt a sense of irritation that somebody should be displaying *his* dump truck for sale. Then he remembered his mission and trudged on along the street.

Suddenly he heard a familiar sound. It could be only one thing: Earless Osdick trying to bark like a dog. He looked about him and then he saw him, imprisoned in a cage with several rabbits.

"They think he's a rabbit," thought Peter to himself. "And *he* thinks he's a dog!"

Then another thought occurred to him:

"What if somebody buys him and cuts him up and makes him into rabbit stew. Or rabbit pie! Poor little Earless. He'd taste *awful!*"

Earless Osdick was jumping up and down inside, looking anxiously at Peter.

"He'd like me to buy him, I guess," Peter thought. "But I haven't got any money. Besides," he told himself crossly. "Why should I have to buy our own cat?"

Then an idea came to him – a very bold and very brilliant idea.

He turned about and trotted back to the stall where he had seen his dump truck. He walked over quite bravely and pulled all his little cars from his pocket. The green stallkeeper looked at him curiously as Peter thrust the pile of cars at him.

"Og!" said Peter. Then he held out his hand.

The stallkeeper turned each toy over and examined it carefully. Then he looked at Peter again. Peter boldly kept his hand out.

"Og!" said Peter again.

The stallkeeper gave him a wary look, but he examined the cars a second time and Peter could see his eyes glittering. Finally he shrugged, reached into a drawer, pulled out a wad of paper money, counted off some bills and gave them to Peter. Peter thrust them into his pocket, nodded brightly, said "Og" for a third time and walked away.

He felt very strange without any of his little cars. Never before in his life had he parted with one, except to his own friends in exchange for another. If there had been any other way of freeing Earless Osdick, Peter would have taken it. But he could think of no other plan and so he made the sacrifice.

Now he walked down the street toward the stall where the rabbits were caged. Once again he decided that boldness was best. Peter was learning quickly that if you move with perfect confidence and no sign of timidity you can usually get away with anything.

He walked straight to the stall and pulled Earless Osdick out of the cage. The cat tried to lick his face but Peter acted just as if they had never been introduced. He walked to the meat counter (for it was obviously a meat counter) and banged Earless Osdick down on it. He pulled the price tag from the cat's neck and laid that on the counter, too, along with his fistful of money. As he did so, he looked at the money for the first time and saw, to his surprise, that it was Play Money of the kind to be found in Penny's Monopoly Game.

The butcher was wearing a white apron with a comic chef's face painted on it and the words COME AND GET IT in bright colours. Peter had seen such an apron before. Father sometimes wore one at barbecue parties.

When the butcher finished serving the green woman next to him he turned his attention to Peter.

"Og," said Peter, who was swiftly learning the language. And then he added, for good measure, "Og-Og."

The butcher looked at him with great suspicion.

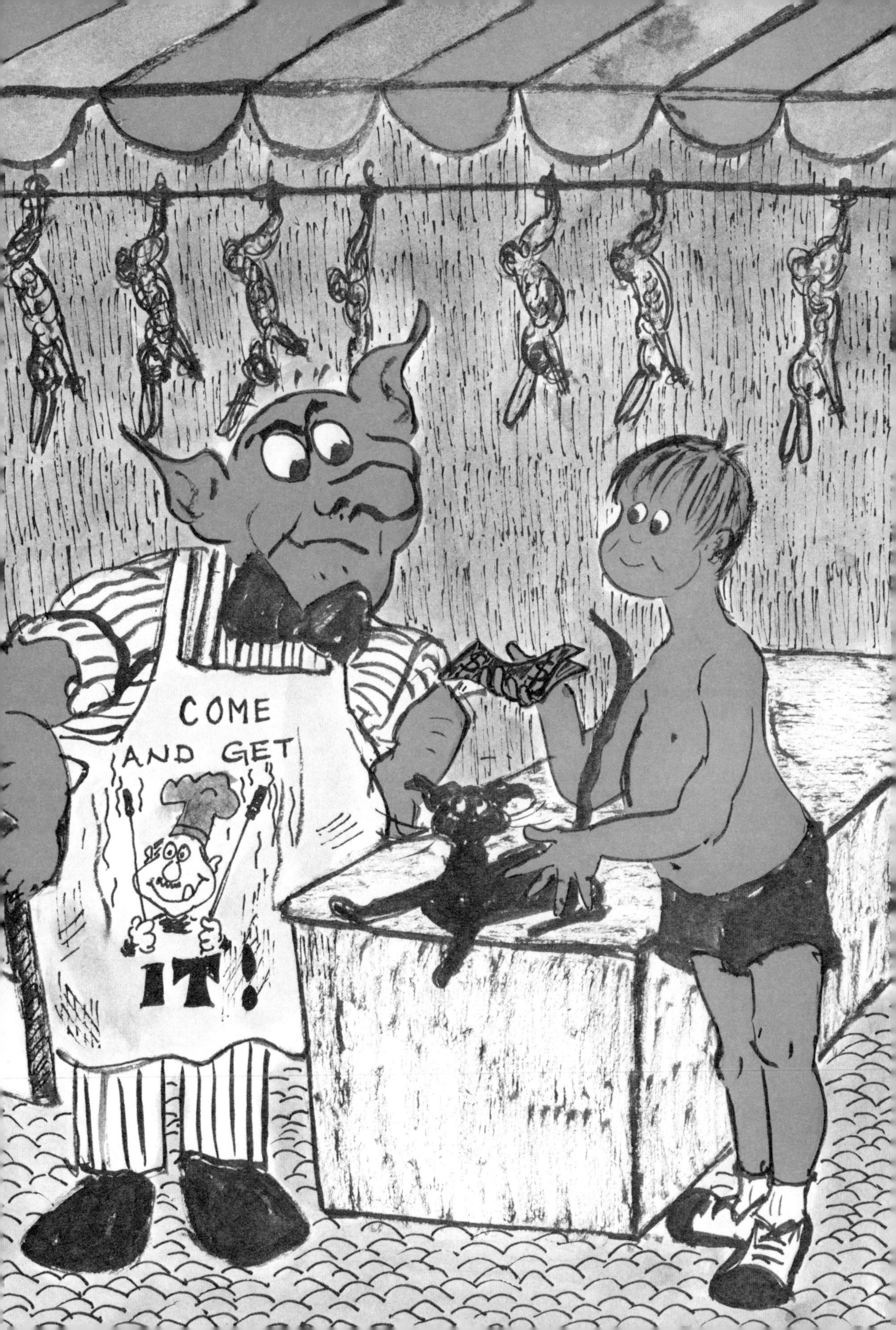
COME
AND GET
IT!

"*Og?*" he said, and Peter noticed that his way of saying it was quite a bit different from his own attempts.

Nonetheless, the butcher counted out some of the money, gave the rest back, then grasped Earless Osdick by the neck and headed for the butcher block where Peter could see an evil-looking cleaver.

Peter reached right over the counter and seized the butcher by his arm before he could chop the cat's head off. The butcher looked at him in surprise and then at his arm where Peter had gripped it. He touched a finger to his arm and then he looked at the finger and then he ran the finger along the white front of the apron: it left a telltale mark of green paint. The butcher seized Peter by the arm and more green paint came off, leaving behind a white streak.

The butcher swung his wicked-looking cleaver, but Peter did not wait. Scooping up Earless Osdick he ducked directly under the stall and then darted up the street. Behind him he could hear a chorus of surprised *Ogs* but he did not wait to see if he was pursued. Clutching the gasping cat by the neck, he threaded in and out through the stalls on the broad main street searching for a hiding place. A small side street crossed the main roadway at right angles and Peter turned up it. Here were a series of orange and yellow houses, shaped like beehives. The second one had an open doorway and Peter dived into it and hid gratefully in the shadows. Outside he could hear the murmur of the crowd but he did not know if they were still chasing him or not. Osdick the cat had wriggled out of his grasp and Peter now stood up to search for him.

"Bang!" cried a voice directly behind him. "You're dead!"

Peter had played cops and robbers for so long that his reaction was automatic. He clutched at his heart and rolled over onto the floor. Then he looked up and saw a small green person peering down at him, holding a tarnished cap pistol in his hand. He was a comical looking figure with an enormous nose and big eyebrows that gave him a look of perfect surprise.

"I gotcha!" said the green man and Peter did not pause to consider it strange that he spoke English.

"You only wounded me," he said. It was what he always said when playing cops and robbers.

"I'm Killer Kane, Scourge of the Underworld," said the green person, impressively. "I'm wanted on three continents."

"I'm Peter," said Peter.

"Oh," said the green man, his eyebrows wiggling. "Peter Rabbit?"

"No," said Peter stubbornly.

"Peter Pan, then," said the green man. "I'm Captain Hook! Avast me hearties and belay!" He looked at Peter for encouragement. "Did I say that right?" he asked.

"Og," said Peter, not knowing what else to say. To tell the truth he was more than a little bewildered by this strange turn of events. The green man did not look like Captain Hook, although he certainly used the proper words.

"Oh, don't start to *og!*" said the green man, making a face. "It's so *boring.* Og-og-og. That's all I get day and night. Avast and belay yuh swabs!" and he made slashing motions with an imaginary cutlass. "Smee! Where are you, Smee? It's Peter Pan we've captured!"

A second green person came out of the shadows. This one was very oddly dressed in a purple gown with spangles on it, but otherwise as green as grass from his long hair to his small green toes. Peter recognized the dress as something Penny had once kept in the Treasure Chest in the Playhouse. She and Pamela took turns wearing it when they were pretending to be Mrs. Finchy de Linch holding a society tea.

"Avast yuh lubber!" cried the man addressed as Smee. Peter suddenly decided to play.

"All right," he said slowly. "I *am* Peter Pan. And – this – " suddenly scooping up Earless Osdick – *"this is the crocodile!* Tic-tic-tic-tic."

Osdick, feeling that he was being put to an important use, bared his teeth like a dog, tried to bark and failed miserably. He did, however, succeed in croaking and that seemed to be effective.

"Not the crocodile!" cried Captain Hook shrinking back against the wall. "Have mercy, mate! Take the beast away and we'll all be friends! I'm only a poor, honest seafaring man, I am, begging yer Honour's pardon!"

He looked so absolutely terrified that Peter, who was very soft-hearted, relented.

"I didn't mean to frighten you," he said.

"It's perfectly all right," said the other cheerfully. "I quite enjoyed it, and you may lay to that. Eh, Smee?"

"Let's all be Indians," said Smee, pushing the hair back from his eyes. "We could shoot up the stagecoach. The crocodile can be my horse, Black Cloud."

"Let's climb the hills and fire on the settlers!" cried Captain Hook in delight.

"No," said Smee looking sober. "There's trouble in the hills. They caught one of our boatmen in the tunnel – tied 'im up they did. He got away though and now we got two of *theirs* in jail."

He paused and looked around darkly: "There's talk of a *lynchin'* bee," he whispered hoarsely.

"Who'd they catch?" asked Peter, who had been listening to all this with interest. It sounded somehow familiar.

"Two *ogs*," said Smee.

"Oh," said Peter, baffled. For a moment he thought they had been talking about Penny and the Pollywog but now he couldn't be sure.

"The little 'un can only crawl," said Smee. "But I hear the big un's a regular she-devil. Put up quite a fight she did. Say, what's that white mark on your arm, pard?"

Peter looked guiltily at the spot where the butcher's thumb had smeared away the green paint.

"It's . . . it's a tattoo," he blurted.

"*Say!*" said Captain Hook, wiggling his eyebrows in admiration, "it's a real keen tattoo. Let's have a look."

But Peter did not like this turn of events. He had an uneasy feeling that there was going to be trouble at the cave and he was also pretty certain that if he stayed much longer in this funny little house with these two strangely playful little men he would be found out.

He reached over and plucked the cap pistol from Captain Hook's hand.

"I'm blasting out!" cried Peter. "The first one to make a move's a dead man."

And, holding Earless Osdick by the neck, he backed out of the house and stealthily made his way into the crowds on the main street once again. In the distance he heard somebody call out "Bang!" but he paid no attention.

The cave he was seeking was somewhere at the far end of the street, he knew, and he set off in that direction. He dug into his pocket for one of his toy cars and realized, with a pang, that he had sold them all to ransom Earless Osdick. Peter never felt properly secure without a pocket full of little cars. He badly wanted his little tractor which was his favourite but his pockets were empty of everything except a small wad of Play Money.

Unconsciously, he held Earless Osdick as if *he* were a car.

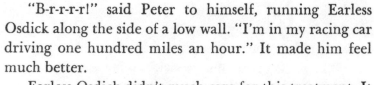

"B-r-r-r-r!" said Peter to himself, running Earless Osdick along the side of a low wall. "I'm in my racing car driving one hundred miles an hour." It made him feel much better.

Earless Osdick didn't much care for this treatment. It wasn't dignified for a dog, he thought – or even for a crocodile. But he had been through quite a lot that afternoon and was so happy to see Peter that he didn't protest.

By now Peter had reached the end of the street. It made an abrupt curve and there, on the right-hand side, dug into the hill, was the cave where Yukon King had indicated Penny was being held.

Peter stood uncertainly for a moment at the mouth of the cave for he was not quite sure what he should do. So far, however, the bold approach had worked and Peter determined to try it again. He strode resolutely into the darkness and then stopped for a moment to get his bearings. As he did so he felt a hard object pressed into his back.

"Reach, pardner!" said a deep voice. "I've got yuh covered. One move and you're a dead hombre."

But Peter had had enough of games.

"That doesn't fool me," he said boldly. "It's a toy gun and it won't even work. Put it down!"

He turned about quite fiercely to find Penny, her eyes wide, shrinking back against the stone wall.

9/Earless Osdick's Secret Mission

Pamela lay daydreaming beneath the patch of giant mushrooms at the top of the ridge overlooking the town of the Ogs. She had quite forgotten where she was. The events of the afternoon had come as less of a surprise to her than to the others for Pamela saw so many strange things with those large brown eyes of hers that she was no longer surprised by small creatures or odd faces. She knew that there was nothing more that could be done for the moment and that it would be foolish for either Patsy or her to show themselves. And so she lay on her back, staring up through the mushroom tops, lost in a world of her own.

She had just about decided what she would be when she grew up. Penny, she knew, was going to be a Captain; she didn't know what she was going to be a Captain of – a baseball team possibly or an army, or maybe an aircraft carrier. Penny said it was time a girl was Captain of *something*: only boys seemed to be captains and that wasn't fair. Patsy had announced that she was going to be a jockey. Pamela, who had doubts about Penny being a Captain, thought that Patsy would probably make it. Peter was going to be a garbage man, replacing the unfortunate Mr. Whipple after he was killed in an accident. But Pamela had different ideas. Pamela had decided that after-

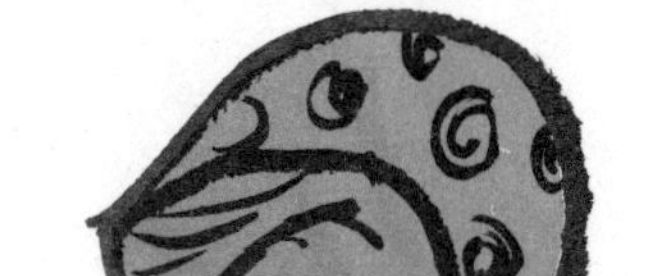

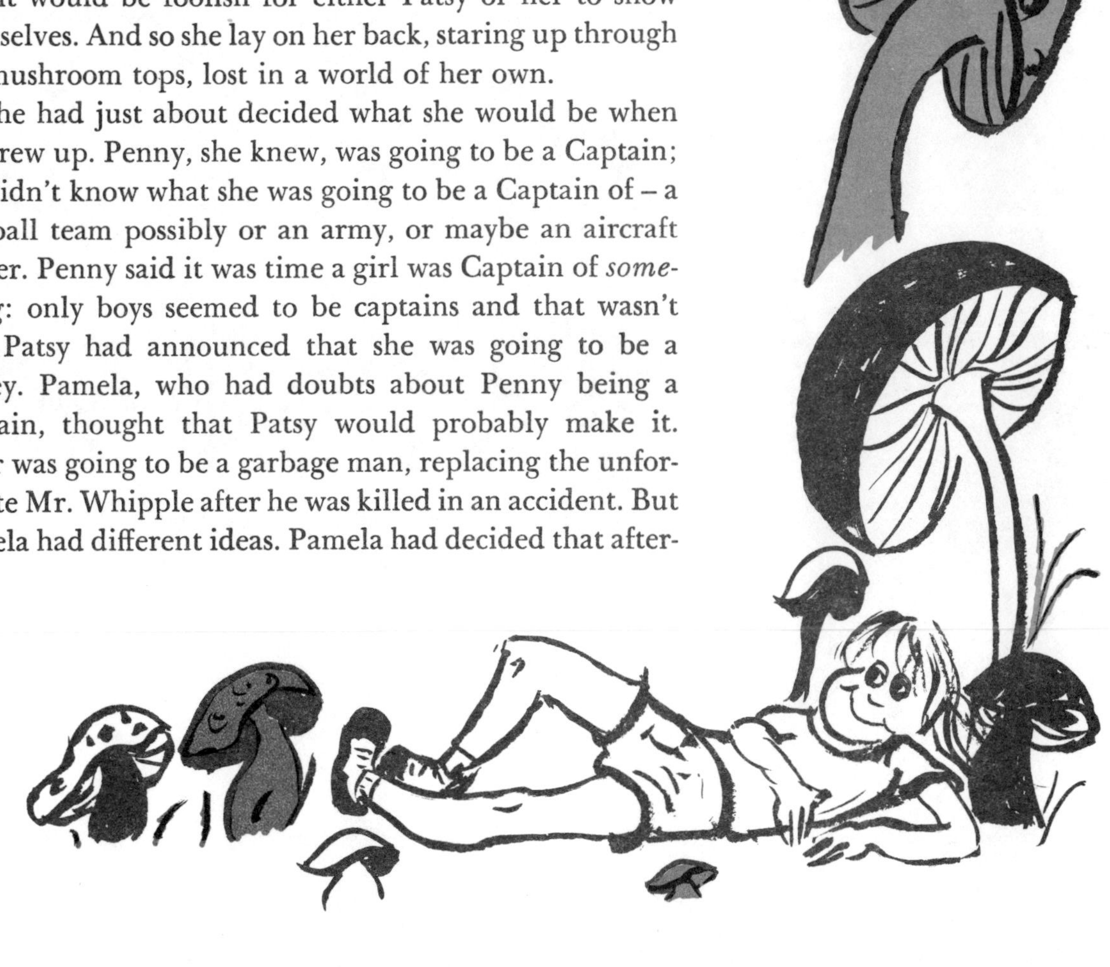

noon that when she grew up she was going to be a Mother.

She would live, she thought, in a small, cosy little house – quite a bit like the Playhouse – and she would have seven children, all of them girls. They would be named after flowers: Daisy, Petunia, Pansy, Rose, Columbine, Marigold, and Tulip. The children would wear party dresses most of the time, with several petticoats, and Pamela would cook for them. Pamela decided that for breakfast they would always have Scrummies, the sugar-coated cereal that tasted like toffee. (They would have seven packages of Scrummies at a time so that *everyone* could have a prize.) For lunch they would have French fried potatoes and for supper Pamela would make a chocolate cake with frilly icing. They would all sleep together in one big bed, she and the seven children, and they would read *Anne of Green Gables* aloud and, on special days, perhaps the *Mad Monster* – though Pamela wasn't sure that small children should be allowed to read comic books, especially a comic book as silly as the *Mad Monster*.

"Pam!" Patsy was shaking her. "I think something's happening!"

While Pamela had been daydreaming, Patsy had been examining the scene below them with lively interest.

She could see the people scurrying up and down the streets and in the small square near the river. On the water, she could see a good many little boats moving about, propelled by green men with long poles. She saw no animals but she spotted several parties far over to the right, climbing up the slopes and chopping down clumps of mushrooms.

"Look, Pam!" she whispered. Not far away a group of workers was dragging a huge mushroom down the slope toward the little town.

"Where do you suppose they're taking it?" Patsy asked.

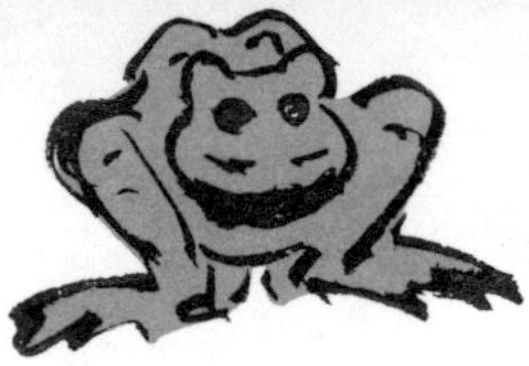
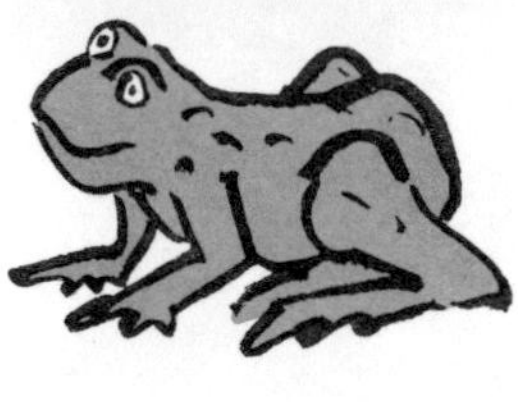

"They're probably going to eat it," said Pamela and the thought made her hungry. She wished she had a heaping bowl of vitamin-rich energy-building Scrummies in front of her, topped with bananas, just like in the advertisements.

The men had reached the bottom of the slope and the two girls saw them hoist the big mushroom on their shoulders and move off down the street with it, like ants at a picnic carrying away a giant bread crumb.

There was a large round building not far away and into this they took the mushroom.

"I s'pose it's some sort of mushroom factory," said Pamela.

She peered off into the darkness to see where the river went but it vanished into a kind of haze, winding in a glittering chain across the landscape. There was no grass anywhere, Pamela noted – only a soft, velvety fungus on the rocks. When you walked on it, it was a bit like treading on a carpet.

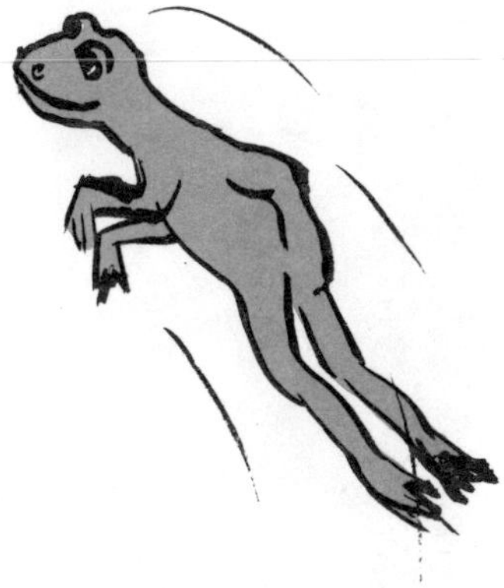

Pamela reached down and peeled some of the fungus off. It was just like cloth.

"Perhaps they make clothes out of it," she said to Patsy.

"I saw a guy wearing doll's clothes," Patsy told her.

"Don't be silly, Patsy," Pamela said.

"No, I really did, Pam. Down below."

"I don't believe it," said Pamela firmly, "though I wouldn't blame them if they did," she added, half to herself. "It looks like a pretty dull place to live. I wonder what they do for fun."

"They probably make up games and things," Patsy said. "You know – like we do." She had taken two toads, a green frog, and Snavely, her pet garter snake, out of her pockets and was playing with them. The reptiles were rather groggy from having been cooped up so long and so

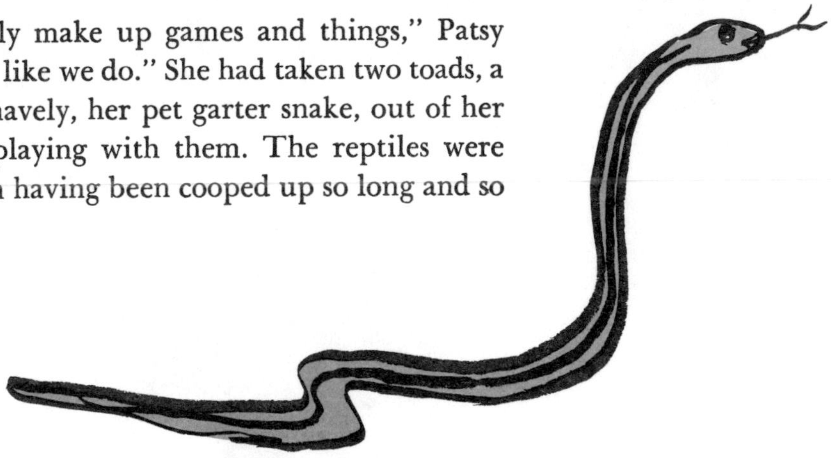

made no attempt to escape. The frog, indeed, had been in Patsy's pocket for almost two days. The night before that he had slept in bed with her. He was feeling quite cranky and out of sorts and would have felt much worse if he hadn't had a nice drink of water during the trip down the river.

Pamela had already started to daydream again. She thought of all the events that had taken place that afternoon: her first sight of the little green man with the saw; the descent down the tunnel and into the river; Penny's disappearance, Yukon King's brilliant detective work, and finally Peter's foray into the village, disguised as a green man.

"What a story we'll have to tell when we get back!" Pamela told herself. Then she thought better of it. Nobody ever believed her when she saw things and they certainly wouldn't believe any of *this*. "Patsy'll probably tell," she thought. "She tells everything. Well, they won't believe *her* either."

"Pam!" Patsy was tugging at her again. "Somebody's coming!" At the same moment Yukon King gave a low growl.

Pamela peered out from between the mushroom stalks and, to her dismay, saw a gang of green people climbing the slope toward their mushroom patch. They were carrying tiny hatchets and she saw that they intended to chop down the very mushrooms they were all hiding under.

"Maybe we could sneak back to the next patch," Patsy was whispering.

"There isn't time: they'll see us!"

"Then what do we *do*?" Patsy said, and Pamela saw that she was about to burst into tears.

"I don't know," said Pamela, feeling the weight of responsibility heavy on her shoulders. Even as she spoke

she could see the green legs of the men showing between the mushroom stalks. In another moment they would start to hack them down . . .

◎ ◎
◎

When Peter turned about and faced Penny in the cave he showed no surprise.

"Hi, Penny," he said.

"Good gracious!" Penny almost shouted. "It's Peter!"

"Pam's up above with Patsy and Yukie. They painted me green. They want you to come now," Peter said, just as if he were bringing a message from Mother that supper was ready.

"Wait, Peter," said Penny, for he had started to march out of the cave. "It's not going to be that easy. It's okay for you – you look like one of them. But Pollywog and I are white – and I'm far too big. We'll have to think of something."

"We could wait till it's dark and then go," Peter suggested.

"It doesn't get dark, silly," Penny said. "There's no sun down here. Just that glow from the river keeps it lit. I bet it's the same all the time."

"Then when do people sleep?" Peter asked.

"How should I know?" said Penny. "Maybe they don't sleep at all in this silly place." But then she remembered that the sheriff had fallen asleep. "Maybe they all sleep at different times," she said. "They don't really seem very organized about anything."

"Let's shoot our way out," said Peter, fiercely.

"Well, it may come to that," Penny told him. "Anyway you take one of these guns."

"That's my old cap pistol," said Peter, taking it and

looking it over carefully. "It's broken," he added. "It wouldn't even shoot a fly."

"They don't seem to know about that," said Penny. "Or at least they don't seem to care. It's like they were all playing a game or something. Maybe they've read so many comic books they think *any* gun will shoot. I bet they've never tried to shoot anybody, really. They've never even had anybody in this old jail before."

As Penny talked, as much to herself as to Peter, it occurred to her that the green people might not be as dangerous to handle as she had at first supposed. Still, she remembered, with a little shiver, two of them had had a very firm grip on her arm! The more she thought about it, the more she believed they must take drastic action.

She began to frown in concentration as she tried to decide on a plan. What would a pirate do? she asked herself. Or Robin Hood or somebody? Then an idea dawned.

"What we need is a hostage," she said to Peter.

"What's a hostage, Penny?"

"Well – it's sort of like a prisoner. What we have to do is capture one of the green people and hold him in front of us. They'll be so afraid we'll hurt him that they'll let us go – I hope," she finished lamely.

She thought for a moment longer.

"He really ought to be somebody important," she said.

"Him?" asked Peter, pointing to the sheriff, reading away at his comic books inside the cell.

"I don't really think he's very important," Penny said dubiously. "Even if he is a sheriff."

"That's my old badge," Peter said suddenly, going over to the cell.

"Give me my badge!" he said, pointing his cap gun at the sheriff. The sheriff unpinned it and meekly handed it over.

"Oh, Peter, you've given me another idea!" Penny said. "*You* can be sheriff!"

"How?"

"Why, take the cowboy hat and the gunbelt and the badge and just walk about. Who'll know the difference? If they're all as dumb as *he* is, you'll get away with it."

"All right," said Peter. "I'd like that." He had achieved two ambitions on this hectic afternoon: first he had finally got himself painted green; now he was going to be a real sheriff, with a hat and a gunbelt. What red-blooded boy could wish for more?

"Now look, Pete," Penny was saying. "The Pollywog and I will stay here. I have a feeling somebody will come soon so don't be any longer than you have to. If anybody *does* come I'll try to stick them up and lock them in the cell. Your job is to find somebody of importance and arrest him. Bring him back here and we'll use him as a hostage."

"How'll I know?" Peter asked.

"Know what?"

"Who's important."

"You'll just *know*. You can always tell important people by the way they walk and the way they act. They *look* important."

"All right," said Peter. "I'll try."

"We really ought to get a message back to Pam, though," Penny said thoughtfully. "She's going to be worried, not knowing what's going on."

"She's at the top," Peter said. "In the mushrooms."

"Yes, but we can't shout at her. If only Yukon King were here he could take a note."

"How about him?" said Peter, picking up Earless Osdick.

"You know, I believe he could!" said Penny. "I'll see if I can get some paper."

She rummaged around and finally tore the back of one of the comic books. Then she looked about for a pencil but there wasn't a sign of any writing instrument in the cave.

"They probably don't know *how* to write," Penny said. "What are we going to do?"

"Some of my paint's still wet," Peter told her. And he smeared his finger across the comic book to show her.

"Well, it'll have to be a short note," Penny said dubiously.

She got a small stick and, using some of the paint, printed across the comic book cover these words:

PAM. WE ARE ALL O.K. WAIT.

"At least that'll make her feel better," she said. "Now, Osdick, here's your chance." And she rolled up the paper and put it in Osdick's mouth.

"Good dog," said Peter, who knew that Osdick hated to be considered a cat. At these words Earless Osdick looked very pleased, and tried to wag his tail.

"Take him outside, Pete," Penny said. "Show him where to go."

Peter took the cat outside and pointed to the mushroom clump on the cliff, high above the cave and slightly off to one side.

"Go find Pam," he said. "That's a good dog."

Off went Earless Osdick, belly down on the ground, as he'd seen his pal, Yukon King, go. He felt very proud that he had been trusted with a vital mission. He pretended that he was a fierce police dog crossing No Man's Land with a message for the Allied General Staff.

"Arf! Arf!" said Osdick to himself, barking like the dog in the comic strips. "Arf! Arf!"

He slipped from boulder to boulder, wriggling under the mushrooms and sliding along the velvety fungus covering, holding Penny's note tightly in his mouth. He was trying to follow Peter's directions but as he had his nose right on the ground and could see very little he wasn't exactly sure *where* he was going. Finally he raised his head up and looked about him. He saw at once that he was lost. Worse than that he was in terrible danger. A group of three or four green men were running toward him, waving hatchets and shouting "Og!" at the top of their voices.

Osdick turned about, intent on escape, but he was too late. A second party of green men had come up from below. One of them reached down and before the little cat could wriggle away seized him by the scruff of the neck and tore the note from his jaws.

"Arf! Arf!" said Osdick, in his boldest voice – but all that really emerged was a rather frightened mew.

10/Remember! I'm a Villain!

Peter was an extremely self-possessed little boy. He almost always did what he was told and he usually did it well. Now he trudged cheerfully out of the prison cave and back to the village again, carefully following Penny's instructions and looking for somebody important.

He did not go back along the main street for he knew that danger lurked in that direction. There were the two playful green people whom he thought of as Smee and Captain Hook. There was the butcher who had noted the green paint on his arm. And somewhere, no doubt raising a hue and cry, was the first green man they had captured in the tunnel and whom Peter still thought of as "Og."

So Peter chose a narrow little street some distance back from the river. The roadway itself was almost empty of people but, through the small windows of the brightly coloured houses, he could see them moving around inside. Several wee green babies were sitting out in the front yards crawling around and saying "Og" the way the Pollywog did and playing with blocks and rubber dolls. Occasionally a green mother would pop out of a house and haul one of the babies inside.

Down at the end of the street, however, Peter could hear a babble of voices. He noticed that the street ended in

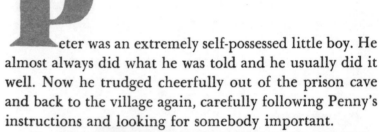

a kind of square and here was a large crowd of grotesquely dressed green people all talking at once. Peter joined them. With his green colour and his large cowboy hat to cover his rather small ears he looked enough like the others to excite no comment.

The crowd had formed a circle around a small group of men. Each of them carried a large green sack, quite empty, and, Peter noticed, several people had stepped up and were giving them money.

Peter decided to risk a question in English. After all, he was a sheriff, and ought to be allowed to talk like one.

He tapped the green man beside him on the shoulder.

"What's up, pardner?" Peter asked him.

"Hi-ya, sheriff," the green man said. "It's another posse headin' up above. I sure hope they do better'n the last one. Pickins been mighty slim recently, and that's a fack."

He seemed to enjoy speaking in cowboy talk, Peter thought to himself: no doubt it got tiresome just saying "Og" all day. He was a round fat little man and he was wearing spectacles which he kept removing from his nose and breathing on and polishing importantly with a corner of a pocket handkerchief. And this was very strange, Peter thought, since the spectacles had no glass in them.

Peter was about to ask another question when a dry withered-up little woman next to the fat man spoke up.

"D'joo see what they brung the las' time? Scrawniest looking critter I ever did see. Some kind of rabbit but no ears on 'im. Had him over t'the butcher counter but I'm dast if I'd buy 'im. D'ruther go back to eatin' mushrooms."

She looked a bit like old Miss Cathcart who lived in the house next to the church, Peter thought. For one thing she had her hair done up in curlers and Miss Cathcart *always* had her hair done up in curlers. Also, Peter noticed, she sighed heavily, just as Miss Cathcart did. If you greeted

Miss Cathcart, politely, by saying "How are you, Miss Cathcart?" Miss Cathcart would never say "Just fine thank you, Peter," as other people almost always did; she would say instead: "Well, I do think I'm just a bit better today," and then she would sigh, just like the little woman.

"I hear the last gang went up above got scairt and come down almost empty handed," the fat man was saying. It was strange to hear him talking like a cowboy, Peter thought, because he did not look or act at all like one. He acted more like Doctor Frableigh, the baby doctor.

"I dew hear they cotched a coupla big ones by mistake," said the old woman.

"I heerd that, too. There'll be all heck to pay over *that*. The rules are you stay away from the big ones. I s'pose yew and th'others got 'em over to the jail, huh, sheriff."

"Yep," said Peter. "We got 'em locked up."

"Goin' t'be a necktie party tonight!" cackled the old woman, looking more and more like Miss Cathcart. She rubbed her hands together with pleasure and Peter shivered a little bit. He wondered if the real Miss Cathcart would also be interested in a necktie party and decided she might have been that day when he and Patsy had eaten some of the green apples from her tree in the back yard.

Peter now decided on a bold question. Truth to tell he was feeling bold. A strange thing was happening to him as he stood in the crowd. He felt much older and more adult than the others around him who really were acting, he thought to himself, like a bunch of small children.

He no longer thought of them as "green people," having become quite used to the colour, but only as a group of rather naughty little boys and girls playing Cowboys and Indians.

He turned to the fat man. "Say, pard," he said, "you seen the boss man around?"

"I guess he'd be up to the big house," the fat man said, carefully polishing the imaginary glass in his spectacles. "But he ought to be down here any moment. He'll want to give the posse some final instructions before it sets out – specially now there's been trouble."

And indeed as he spoke there was a brief murmur and several people stepped back to let somebody through. Peter recognized him at once, just as Penny had said he would, as an Important Person. He, too, wore a pair of black horn-rimmed spectacles without glass in them to which were attached false eyebrows, a comic nose and a black moustache. Some of the kids had worn exactly such a disguise the previous Hallowe'en. He looked so funny that Peter almost laughed out loud at the sight of him. But he noticed that the others stood back very respectfully to let him pass. They obviously didn't find the comic nose funny at all; on the contrary, this curious disguise seemed to make its wearer more important than anyone else. In a strange way, it also made him seem more sinister. He was sort of like a bandit wearing a mask, thought Peter.

As he passed the old woman, the creature suddenly spoke.

"Good morning, madam," he said with a courtly bow. "How are you today? Well, I trust?"

"He's showing off his new lingo," the fat man whispered in Peter's ear. "Gets it from his book learnin'."

"Well, I do think I'm just a bit better today, Chief," said the little old woman.

"She always says that," the fat man said and Peter nodded knowingly.

The Chief – as the little old woman had called him – now elbowed his way to the posse of men in the centre of the square and engaged them in earnest conversation. Peter tried to catch what it was they were saying but he

couldn't hear. He moved forward a little, squeezing in beside a small green person with an impish face. Peter recognized him at once.

"Hi, Og," he said without thinking.

Og, hearing his voice, whirled about at once but did not place his man, for Peter had pulled his sheriff's hat low over his face and nipped around behind a group of chattering women. Og was looking about suspiciously but Peter slowly sidled away.

"Congratulations on your promotion, old boy," said a voice at his side.

Peter turned and looked directly into the face of Captain Hook.

"I really think the sheriff's post is a higher honour than that of Peter Pan," said Captain Hook, wiggling his eyebrows. "I must say you seem to be destined for these heroic roles. They are, I might say, not to my taste. I much prefer to be the villain."

He came up close to Peter, gave him a conspiratorial look, and hissed in his ear.

"At the moment," he whispered, "I am none other than Artful Artie, the Gentleman Pickpocket. See, I have just stolen all your money."

And he triumphantly produced a wad of Play Money which he had neatly filched from Peter's pocket.

"You can keep it," Peter said. He did not much like the way things were turning out.

"A thousand thanks, old boy," said Captain Hook (for Peter still thought of him in the pirate's role) . "Don't give me away now, will you? Not a word to anyone!"

"Not a word," promised Peter.

"Then," said the other, " I won't give *you* away. For you see I know exactly who you are. You're *white!*"

"Oh," said Peter. "Well, don't tell."

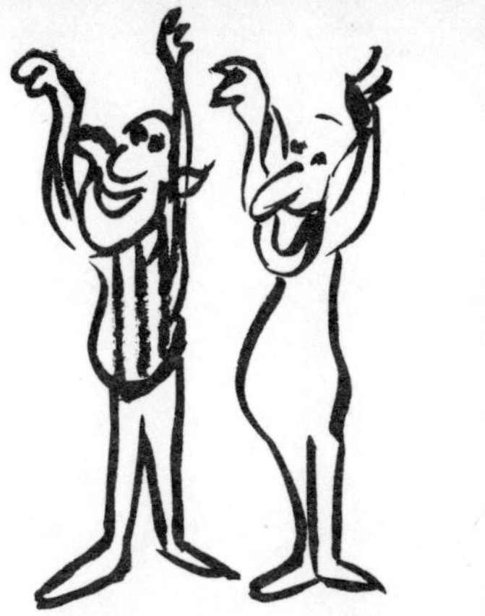

"I shan't," said Captain Hook and then he gave Peter an evil leer. "Not yet a while anyway. I shall let you worry, a bit. Remember, *I'm a villain!*" And he made a horrible grimace at Peter and vanished into the crowd.

All the time, Peter dimly realized, the man with the comic mask, the Chief, had been making some sort of speech in the centre of the square. Peter craned his neck over the heads of the others and saw that Og was now standing beside the Chief.

". . . and so," the Chief was saying, "because of the recent trouble, the posse will not go up through the tunnel today. All movement has been stopped by my order until the crisis is over. Now, I have just been informed, there is a spy amongst us – in this very crowd . . ."

A buzz of alarmed talk rippled through the people. Everybody began to look around and Peter, not to be caught, began to look around too, as if trying to find the spy.

"I will have that translated for those who cannot speak the new tongue," said the Chief, pompously. He motioned another green man who began to speak:

Og!" he cried. "Og . . . og-og-og . . . *og og*. . . ."

Again there was a buzz of noise and people began to look around them suspiciously.

"Where is the sheriff?" cried the Chief, as the interpreter finished. "He is wanted at once."

"The sheriff! The sheriff!" the crowd began to cry.

Peter began to slink back into the crowd but it was too late.

"Here he is, Chief!" cried a familiar voice. "Here is the noble sheriff. He will catch the wicked spy! . . . Won't you, sheriff?" cackled Captain Hook, pushing the reluctant Peter forward into the crowd.

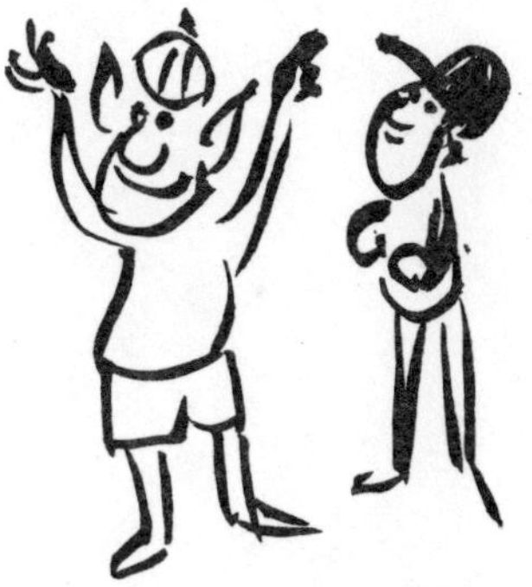

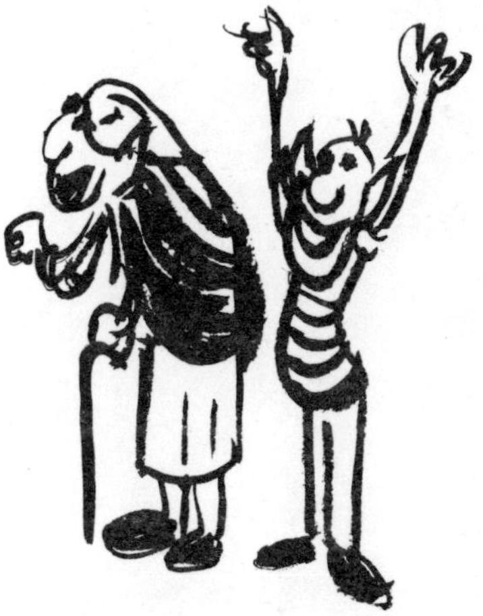

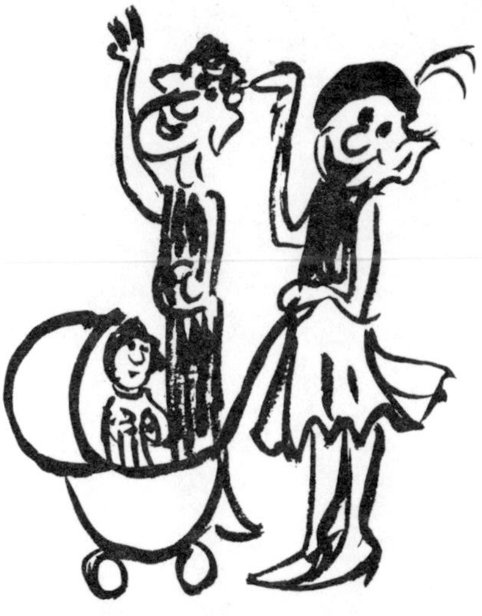

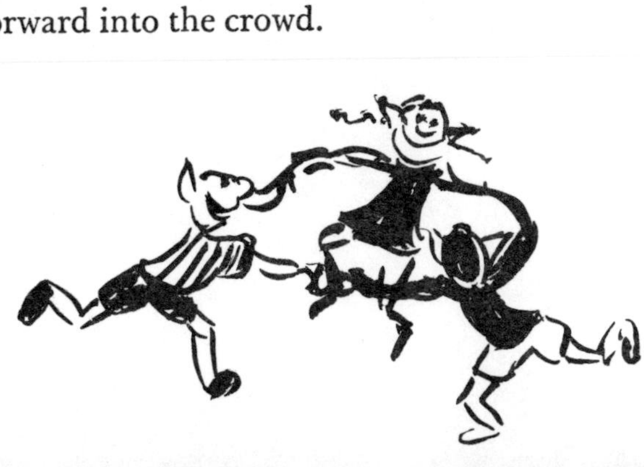

Pamela and Patsy, cowering under the mushroom covering, could have reached out and touched the legs of the green men preparing to hack down their shelter.

Pamela had now decided that the only course open to them was to flee back toward the tunnel in the cliff when the first axe blow struck the mushroom stalk. She placed her lips against Patsy's ear and whispered these instructions to her. Patsy nodded and the two girls made ready to move.

But the blow did not fall. Instead Pamela heard a chorus of *Og*'s and the legs moved several feet away. Very cautiously Pamela poked her nose out of the mushroom clump to try to see what was happening.

The group of green men were gathered in a knot, chattering to themselves and pointing at something farther down the cliff. Pamela, taking advantage of their preoccupation, craned as far forward as she dared, to see what it was they were watching.

Her eye was almost immediately attracted by a sharp quick movement below: something black was wriggling up the side of the slope, standing out clearly against the subdued pastels of the fungus and the bright colours of the rocks and mushrooms. In this strange underground world, Pamela realized, nothing that was natural was black – or white either for that matter.

There was something very familiar about the creature below and Pamela quickly recognized it as Earless Osdick. He had something in his mouth, she saw. He apparently did not realize that he was being watched, for he crept, belly down, from rock to rock and clump to clump, zig-

114

zagging this way and that backwards and forwards across the slope.

The green men were all talking at once; that is to say they were all shouting the one word "Og!" in various tones of voice at each other.

Osdick, his nose flat against the ground, kept on moving erratically up the slope.

"He's going to bump right into them," Patsy whispered in Pamela's ear. But there was no way the girls could warn the cat.

A second party of green men, working at some distance along the ridge, had been attracted by the chatter and they too had seen Osdick. Several of them clambered along the side of the slope, intent on capturing him.

At this point Osdick suddenly sat up, shook his head and looked about him in confusion. Both groups advanced on him, shouting. Osdick turned about but it was too late. A round little man picked him up by the neck and a gnarled little man removed the note from his mouth.

The men now moved back up to the ridge, sat down and began to puzzle over the piece of paper they had taken from Osdick's mouth.

"Pam. We are all O.K. Wait," the gnarled little man read out in a singsong voice.

The two little girls stared at each other in surprise. It was the first time either of them had heard a green man say anything but "Og."

"Pamweareallokwait?" asked the round little man, saying it all at once.

The gnarled man nodded.

"I don't get it," said one of the others.

"It's some sort of secret code!" muttered another, looking around darkly.

"Spies, huh?" said the round little man.

They all nodded and then each man looked over his shoulder as if expecting to see a spy standing behind him.

"Well," thought Pamela, a little relieved, "at least the others are safe."

"Let's have a spy hunt!" cried the gnarled man.

All the little men dropped their axes, clapped their hands together gleefully at this suggestion, and began shouting "Og! Og! Og!" in unison. Then they got down on all fours and began to crawl about, picking up small stones and peering under them and poking their noses around mushrooms and generally sniffing about like police dogs.

Pamela had difficulty in stifling a giggle. A few moments before she had been quite terrified of these fierce-looking figures with their green leathery skins and their big staring eyes and their sharp white teeth. Now they seemed more like children, about Peter's age, playing games of make-believe in a make-believe world.

Patsy, beside her, was trembling with excitement. "Spy" was a game she greatly enjoyed playing and she felt just a bit left out of things. Peter and Penny and Paul, she thought to herself, were having all the adventures while she was stuck in an old mushroom patch with nothing to do. It wasn't fair.

She looked around for Hoppy, her pet frog, but she couldn't locate him. Then she saw he had hopped out from under the mushroom cover and was advancing, a leap at a time, along the ridge.

She tugged at Pam and the two girls watched in fascination as Hoppy advanced upon one of the unsuspecting men. It was the round little man, the one shaped like a small green ball, who had first seized Osdick.

The little man, still on all fours, was creeping along the edge of the ridge, a look of fierce concentration on his

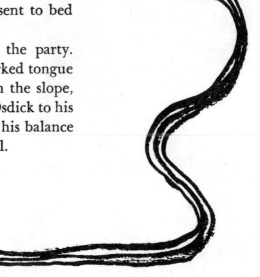

face. Hoppy was no more than two inches from his nose when the little man looked up into the frog's face.

"Hoppy thinks the Greenie's a frog!" Patsy whispered.

The green man emitted a startled yell and reeled back, tumbling all over himself as Hoppy took a friendly jump toward him. Then he leaped to his feet and clambered up the hill toward the others.

All the green men were in a cluster now and all were backing slowly away from Hoppy.

"It's a dragon!" said one in terror.

"It's a monster," quavered another.

"Maybe it's the Mad Monster," said a third, and they all shivered and clung to one another.

Patsy reached into her pocket, pulled out Snavely, the garter snake, and tossed him out beside the frog.

Snavely blinked twice, shot his tongue out a couple of times, and then began to wriggle toward the green men.

The group of would-be spy hunters now began to shriek in terror at the sight of the snake.

"It's come!" one of them cried. "It's happened!"

"Come on," cried Patsy, rising to her feet. "We've got 'em scared!"

"Patsy! *Don't!*" said Pamela.

But Patsy was out from behind the mushroom patch before Pamela could stop her. She scooped up Snavely and waved him at the green men.

She had done it to Mother once, Pamela remembered, and after Mother recovered Patsy had been sent to bed with only crackers for supper.

Patsy's appearance completely unnerved the party. When the snake began to shoot out his red forked tongue they turned tail and began to scramble down the slope, half falling as they went, and leaving Earless Osdick to his own devices. The round little man quite lost his balance and actually rolled down the hill like a football.

Patsy scooped up Hoppy the Frog and crammed him back into her pocket.

"C'mon, Pam!" she cried. "We've got 'em on the run."

"Patsy! Come back!" said Pamela. But she knew it was no good. When Patsy was this way there was no holding her. She was a holy terror.

Patsy uttered a blood-curdling war whoop, which she and the Terrible Twins had been practising for some time, and darted off down the slope waving Snavely.

"We'd better follow," said Pamela with a sigh. But Earless Osdick and Yukon King were already off with Patsy in wild pursuit of their quarry. Moving more carefully, and surely, Pamela brought up the rear.

Patsy had no clear idea of what she intended to do when she got to the bottom. But she had been sitting under the mushrooms quite long enough and the release from this prison went to her head like a tonic. She was in her element – her pigtails streaming behind her and her face glowing with the chase as she half tumbled, half scampered down the velvety slopes.

11/The Shooting of Captain Hook

In the square in the middle of the town, every eye was turned on Peter as, his ten-gallon hat pulled low over his eyes, he advanced unwillingly toward the centre of the crowd.

"Sheriff!" said the Chief, importantly, adjusting his comic nose, "do your duty! There's a spy amongst us. Indeed, I have reason to believe that the city is crammed with spies!"

And he looked around mysteriously and imposingly to make sure that his words had effect. "They are everywhere!" he said in a hoarse whisper. The crowd murmured and drew together, each man eyeing his neighbour suspiciously.

"Come, come, sheriff," said the Chief, impatiently. "Have you caught the spy yet?" He reminded Peter of Freddie Frith, a boy he sometimes played with who was always being bossy.

"Not yet," said Peter, not knowing what else to say.

He saw Captain Hook on the edge of the crowd grinning cheerfully at him. Well, thought Peter, if he wants to be a villain he might as well be a real one.

"*He's* the spy!" Peter said, pointing at Captain Hook.

"I might have known it!" exclaimed the Chief. "Fine

police work, sheriff! Don't move, spy! The sheriff has an itchy trigger finger."

Far from being upset by this turn of events, Captain Hook looked positively delighted.

"How did you trap me?" he asked, raising his hands above his head and bounding forward. "I'm a master spy," he said to the Chief.

"Take him to the jail, sheriff," said the Chief. "The crowd's getting ugly."

"Tell them to go home," said Peter.

"Disperse!" cried the Chief in a thundering voice. "Translate that!" he added, turning to the interpreter.

"OG!" shouted the interpreter and the crowd began to melt away.

"C'mon," said Peter, and the three of them – Peter, Captain Hook and the Chief – headed down the street toward the cave which served as a jail. As they reached the entrance Peter turned to the Chief.

"I forgot," he said mildly. "You're a hostage. Stick 'em up." And he poked his cap pistol in the green man's midriff.

The Chief looked startled and raised his hands.

"I'm the *real* spy," Peter said, proudly.

"Oh, no, you're *not!*" said Captain Hook. "That's not a bit fair. *I'm* the spy. You said I could be, you know. You *promised.*"

"No," said Peter, "it's my turn, now." And he marched the two of them into the cave where Penny, in an absolute frenzy of anxiety, was awaiting them.

As Peter entered, he noticed that the Pollywog had somehow got back inside the cell again and was tearing up the real sheriff's comic books, much to the green man's annoyance.

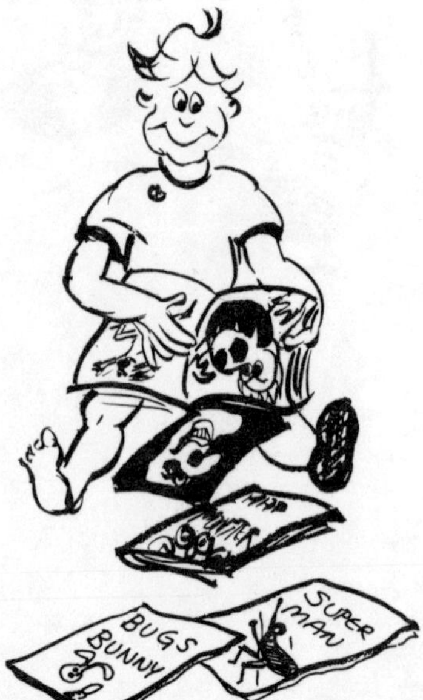
MAD
BUGS BUNNY
SUPER MAN

"Here's the hostage, Penny," Peter said. "I brought two."

"Oh, I *like* being a hostage," burbled Captain Hook. "I don't believe I've ever been a hostage before."

"That's not fair!" shouted the Chief. "*I'm* the hostage. He said I was!" and the two queer green people began to quarrel among themselves.

"Who is he?" Penny asked Peter, pointing to the Chief.

"Boss," said Peter. "I think he *likes* being stuck up."

"Well," said the Chief, conversationally, "it does relieve the monotony, you know."

"Are you really the boss of all this?" Penny asked.

"Definitely," the green man answered importantly. "Actually my real title, handed down from generation to generation, is the Grand Exalted Keeper of the Holy Mushroom Patch — or, if you prefer the original language, Og, Og-Og-Og *Og*."

"Oh!" said Penny.

"Only there *is* no Holy Mushroom Patch," the Grand Exalted Keeper added. "We ate it. That was during the Great War with the Ogs."

"The Ogs?"

"They live across the river. We used to fight a lot for something to do. Of course, since we got the tunnels working there's no more need."

"I don't understand all of this," said Penny. "Who are you anyway — and how long have you lived down here?"

"Who *are* we?" said the Chief, in surprise. "Well, I like *that!* We're — we're *us!*"

"Who are *you*, for that matter?" asked Captain Hook.

"I'm Penny," said Penny.

"I'm Peter," said Peter, politely.

"But — if the people across the river are called Ogs —

then what are you people called?" Penny wanted to know.

"We haven't got any name," the Chief said. "They call *us* Ogs, for that matter."

"It's the only word we have, you see," said Captain Hook, a bit apologetically.

"But now we have the new language we've all got separate names," the Chief said. "Just like you. It's ever so much more fun! At the moment I'm Wyatt Earp. I got it out of *Classic Comics*. I think it's quite a nifty name, don't you?"

"What do you mean, *at the moment?*" Penny asked.

"Oh, well, we change a lot. I mean it would be very selfish of me to use Wyatt Earp *all* the time. Somebody else will want it."

"One week," said Captain Hook wistfully, "one week I was that villain Jesse James! Tell me, what is Jesse James really like? I mean, *really?*"

"How should I know?" said Penny. The conversation, she felt, was getting off on a very queer tack indeed.

"But don't you live up there with him?"

"Not *with* him, silly. He's in books. Besides, I'm sure he must have been dead for years and years."

"Dead!" the Captain looked shocked and Penny thought he was going to cry. "You mean some hombre outdrew him? They had oughta strung him up!" And he clenched his fists tightly in anger and sorrow.

"He died with his boots on," said Peter, who knew all about Jesse James.

"It all happened years ago," Penny said. She was a little vague as to when it actually *had* happened. "Probably a hundred years ago!" she added, guessing.

It was the others' turn to look confused, and Penny seized the chance to ask her question again:

"How long have you people lived down here?"

"How long? Why – *always*. This is where we *live*."

"But why? Why don't you live up above like everybody else?"

"Well, everybody else *doesn't* live up above," the Chief said. "There are plenty down here, you know. All along the big river – and probably many more on smaller branches we don't know about."

"But if you're so crazy for comic books and toys and funny hats and things, why don't you just come up and live like the rest of us?" Penny persisted.

The Chief gave her a queer look.

"You don't really mean that," he said finally.

"Of course I mean it."

"You wouldn't like us up there at all," said the little man. "We're green, you know. We're different."

"Well, for Heaven's sakes," Penny said, exasperated. "We've got all colours up above, too. We haven't anybody green but we have them white and brown and yellow and black. So there!"

"And how are these people treated?" the little green man said.

"Well," said Penny uneasily, "it all depends, I guess."

"That's why we stay down here," the little man said.

Penny didn't at all like the trend of this talk. But she did see the green man's point.

"I guess the poor little things wouldn't have a very good time of it up above at that," she told herself. "At school the big boys would laugh at them."

"But the tunnels?" she asked, trying to change the subject, "why do you have the tunnels?"

"You built a building right on top of one," said the Chief petulantly. "That wasn't fair, you know. It's difficult enough as it is to keep them from filling up with mud and snow."

"Can't you start from the beginning – about the tunnels?" Penny asked.

"Well, in the beginning we didn't *have* tunnels," the Chief said. "In the old days we lived down here without any kind of contact with the world above."

"And *oh*, was it dull!" said Captain Hook mournfully.

"Yes," said the Chief, "it *was* dull. The only cloth we had to wear was the skin we scraped off the rocks. The only food we had were the mushrooms."

"Ugh! Those mushrooms!" said Captain Hook making a face.

"I like mushrooms," Peter said.

"Well, you wouldn't if that's *all* you had," the Chief said. "Why, we had mushroom porridge, mushroom stew, mushroom cake, mushroom pie, mushroom soup, mushroom candies, mushroom cookies, mushroom salad, mushroom milk, mushroom omelette, mushroom gruel . . ."

"Nourishing, mind you!" cried Captain Hook, with a horrible wink. "Full of rich, juicy vitamins, and all that . . ."

"Like eating Pablum all day," said Peter, sympathetically.

"We built things out of dry mushroom stalks," the Chief continued. "When properly prepared they are rather like a very light wood. We still use them a good deal."

"What did you do for fun?" Penny asked.

"There *wasn't* any fun!" cried Captain Hook, raising his eyebrows and lowering them again. "We didn't know about fun! All we did was eat mushrooms and talk to ourselves in that awful language: Og Og Og all day long."

"Why didn't you invent other words?" Penny asked.

"We didn't know we could," said the Chief. "Besides, you know, it's very much easier to learn things if you only have one word. It made school very simple. Spelling was simple! Grammar was only slightly more difficult."

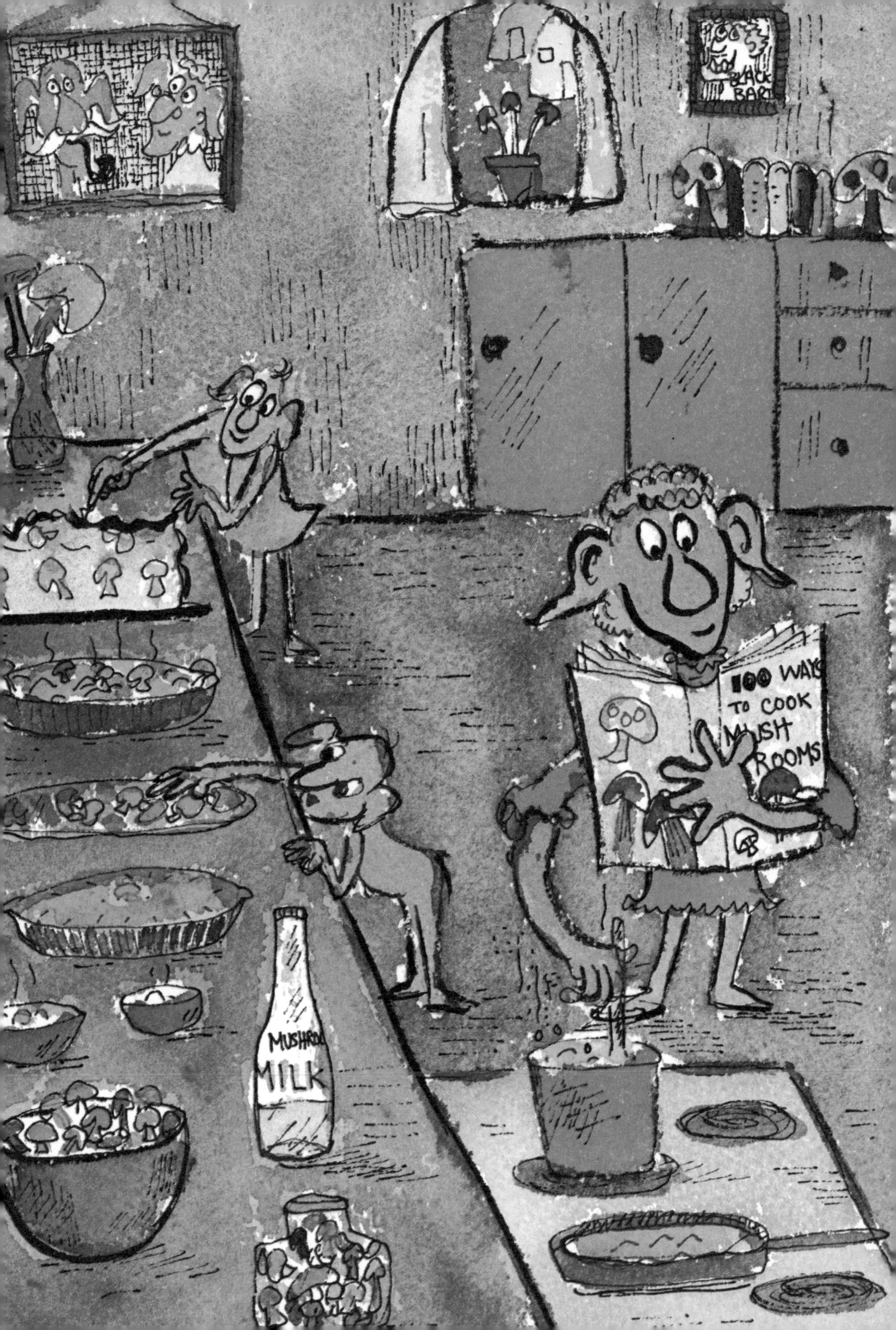
BLACK BART
100 WAYS TO COOK MUSH ROOMS
MILK

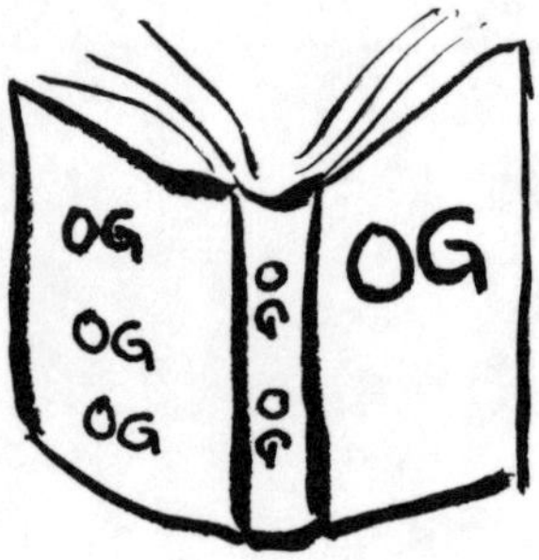
OG
OG
OG
OG
OG
OG

"I was *very* bad at grammar," said Captain Hook sadly. "I could never understand that the plural of Og was Og or that the objective of Og was also Og. Nor did I ever understand, I fear, that the first person singular of the verb Og was Og while the third person plural was also Og. As for the subjunctive – I never could master it."

"History," said the Chief, ignoring him, "was summed up in a single word, 'Og!' Thus the history books contained only one page with this one word on it and the course was taught completely, including memory work and revisions, in not much more than six months."

"*I* would think it wouldn't take much more than a day," said Penny. "Or maybe an *hour*."

"We like to be thorough down here," said the Chief. "Besides, there was recess."

"Recess?"

"It was five months long."

"Oh, how lovely!" cried Penny. "Imagine having five whole months of recess!"

"But, do you see, there was absolutely nothing to do!" exclaimed Captain Hook. "If you think it's fun to go around all day long eating mushrooms and saying 'Og' to everybody you are terribly wrong. Have you ever tried to get an idea across using the one word 'Og'? It is extremely difficult. I know a lot of people still use the language but they are lazy and lack imagination. I, for one, prefer to speak the majestic and rolling tones of those great Englishmen, Ebenezer Scrooge, Robinson Crusoe, Captain Hook, Wild Bill Hickock and Garth Greatheart!"

"How did you come to learn it at all?" Penny asked.

"It happened," said the Chief, "that one day a party of men worked their way up the river in a mushroom boat – well above the waterfall. Nobody had been there before because people were afraid of a Thing that they said lived away up there."

"What kind of Thing?" Penny asked.

"I'm coming to that. Life was so boring, finally, that a group of these men decided to have an adventure and go in search of the Thing. It turned out to be a small brown animal who'd dug a hole right down to the river. It was just as afraid of them as they were afraid of it."

"Sounds like a gopher," Penny said. "Or a mole."

"Well, whatever it was, it had dug all the way down. The men who found the tunnel – for this was the first of the tunnels – clawed their way up until they came out into your world. They brought back some souvenirs they found lying around on the ground. They're in our museum now."

"What kind of souvenirs?"

"Oh, a nail, for one thing. And a comb. And an old straw hat. They caused an absolute sensation when they were first placed on exhibit. After that the tunnel was used regularly. Some of the people learned to snare rabbits and that was mainly what we went after. We ate mushrooms with rabbit sauce. Yum! Yum!"

"Most people would say it was rabbit with mushroom sauce," Penny told him.

"It all depends what you're used to," the Chief said.

"Then what happened?" said Penny, entranced at the story.

"Well, the thing got organized as time went on. Companies were formed to exploit the tunnels – for several more were quickly dug. Then there were trading companies formed to send expeditions to the top. We could only go at certain times: usually when it was dark up above, and only when it was warm.

"As the men grew more experienced they began to find all sorts of things lying around in the grass and in the woods. When they found the first picture book – well, you can imagine the excitement!"

"That was how we learned to talk like you," the little man said, "by studying the pictures. And sometimes the explorers would listen to your people as they played their games – being cowboys and things."

"Those would be children," Penny exclaimed.

"Oh? We didn't know. Are you children?"

"Yes, of course."

"How interesting. I thought you were very old and grown up."

"Thank you," said Penny. "I'm *almost* grown up," she added quickly. And certainly she felt very grown up at this point.

"Well," said the Chief, "things became much more lively after the tunnels were properly organized. Now as you see we have everything down here that you have in your world. We really are extremely modern and up-to-date, you know."

He sounded very proud of it all and Penny didn't have the heart to explain that all they really had were cast-off toys and books left lying around by careless children.

("I suppose," she thought, "that the reason they talk mainly about comic book characters is that children don't usually leave *good* books lying around outside." She wondered if the green men had read *Treasure Island* in its original version or *The Count of Monte Cristo*. Captain Hook would certainly enjoy those, she thought, and she made a mental note to leave a couple of old copies lying about in a conspicuous place – if she ever got back home again.)

"We act just like you people, too," the Chief was explaining smugly. "It's much more fun, you know, to pretend to be something you aren't."

"Yes," said Penny, truthfully. "I know." And she thought of the Pollywog, Earless Osdick and Yukon King, all pretending like mad. And then she thought of herself

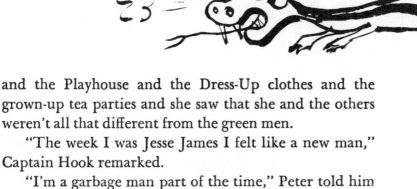

and the Playhouse and the Dress-Up clothes and the
grown-up tea parties and she saw that she and the others
weren't all that different from the green men.

"The week I was Jesse James I felt like a new man,"
Captain Hook remarked.

"I'm a garbage man part of the time," Peter told him
sociably.

Another question occurred to Penny.

"Do you always go *up* the river?"

"Oh, always!"

"Wouldn't it be easier to go down?"

"Oh, no one ever goes *down*," the Chief told her.
"That's where the Snake People live."

"The Snake People?"

"Yes, terrible slithery monsters with beady eyes and
forked tongues and slavering jaws."

"If you've never been down, how do you know?"

"Oh, we've heard stories," said the Chief darkly.

"What stories? From whom?"

"Why, our fathers and mothers told us. And their
fathers and mothers told them. We've got a big net across
the river below so the snake people can't swim up and
attack us."

"How do you know it's not just another bit of imagination, like the Thing who turned out to be a gopher – or
something?" Penny asked him.

"You just don't understand!" the Chief said, shaking
his head. "This is *real!*" And he shuddered a little at the
thought of the terrible Snake People.

"Well," said Penny politely, not wanting to make a big
issue of it, "thank you for telling us your story. Now it's
getting late and we'll have to go."

"Go?" said the little man.

"Yes, we have to go home for supper, now," Penny said.

"Oh, you can't go," the Chief said firmly. "You'd tell.

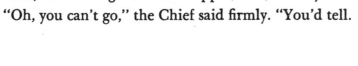

You'll have to stay down here."

"Tell? You mean about all of you?"

"Exactly. Then we'd have parties of tourists prowling around down here, staring at us, peering into our houses and poking us with sticks. Oh, no – that would never do. No, no! we can't have that. I won't be poked at by tourists."

"Well, we won't tell," Penny said. "Anyway, we're going whether you like it or not!" Now that she knew more about the green Ogs, Penny was much less afraid of them.

"You'll never make it alive!" said Captain Hook, once more slipping into comic book talk. "I shall do something dashing and desperate, I warn you. I can be *very* desperate, you know!"

And he assumed what he considered to be his desperate look – grimacing and hissing between his teeth, and clenching and unclenching his small fists and rolling his eyes horribly beneath his enormous green eyebrows.

"We're taking you both with us as hostages," Penny said firmly, not in the least worried by the excitable green man.

"I knew no good would come of this," the Chief muttered. "It's all the fault of Garth Greatheart!"

"Garth Greatheart!" Penny wished Pamela were here to hear this.

"He's the one who insisted on cutting the hole in the floor of your house. He said it would be full of wonderful things. I warned him – but, oh no! he wouldn't listen to my wise counsel. He thought you'd all gone out and when he saw the rabbit without the ears he decided to snatch it first. Then the other animal fell in so they took them both. He sold the rabbit but the other animal made such a terrible noise we were afraid of it so we locked it up. We were going to pretend he was a monster; it would have been good fun, but it's all spoiled now."

"C'mon," said Pete, shoving the cap pistol in his ribs.

But just as he spoke there was a terrifying commotion outside the door of the cave. Several green people went rushing past in stark terror. To her astonishment Penny saw that Patsy was following in hot pursuit. Yukon King and Earless were right behind, both trying to bark like the big dogs on television.

"Patsy!" screamed Penny, "you come right back here!"

"There's no use shouting at her when she's this way!" said Pamela, strolling quietly into the cave. "She'll slow down in a moment."

Outside the cave, now, a crowd of green people was beginning to gather. Suddenly, while the children's attention was diverted, Captain Hook made a plunge for the door.

"Bang! Bang!" shouted Peter, whirling around and pointing the cap pistol at him. "Bang! Bang! You're dead."

Captain Hook twisted about, staggered, pressed his hand to his heart, made a gurgling noise in his throat and slowly sank to his knees. It was his finest moment, as Penny said later.

"Yuh got me, pardner!" he croaked, as he tumbled over. He twitched a bit and then lay perfectly still.

"Oh, Peter," said Pamela. "You've killed him!"

From the thickening crowd outside the cave an angry murmur began to rise.

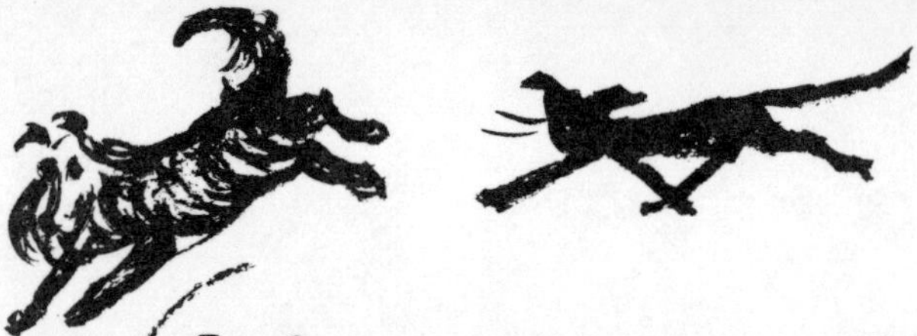

12/Patsy's Adventures with Snavely

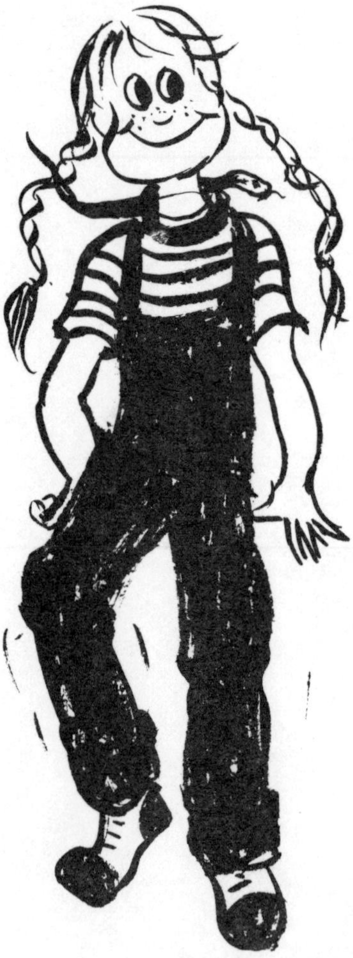

Patsy and the two animals kept right on running past the cave and on around the curve in the hillside. As Pamela had said, once Patsy got going it was hard to stop her. It took a while before she ran down like a clockwork toy, slowed to a trot and then to a walk, and finally sat down on the roadside panting heavily.

The green people had jumped out of her way as she ran. Some of them had dashed into the little houses to hide. For certainly Patsy made a strange sight with her pigtails flying behind her and the two strange animals dashing along beside her, and Snavely the garter snake sticking his tongue out at everyone.

When Patsy sat down, the street was empty. She looked about to get her bearings and realized that she was lost. She had dashed right through the village – or more properly, around it – and was now somewhere on the far side.

In the distance she could see the cataract tumbling from the black hole high up in the cliffside, and so she decided that was as good a place as any to head for. On the way, she told herself, she might just have an adventure.

"C'mon, Yukon King – c'mon, Earless," she said, "and you, too, little Snavely." And she wound the snake around her neck so he'd be safe.

When they reached the first house on the outskirts of the village, Patsy decided to look inside for she had difficulty in passing *anything* with an opening in it. She was always peering into boxes and cupboards. When she was smaller, her mother had great difficulty in stopping her from going into strange people's houses.

When Patsy peeked into the opening she saw a group of green people seated on benches around a low table. The walls were covered with the same kind of fuzzy material that grew all over the ground and the rocks. There were three pictures, all framed neatly: one of Donald Duck, one of Tom and Jerry, the cat and mouse team, and one of Black Bart. They were all covers torn from comic books; the idea appealed to Patsy who decided she would try to frame some for her room when she got home.

The green man at the head of the table was carving half of a giant mushroom, rather like a turkey, and Patsy could smell the delicious odour of roast mushroom pervading the small room. It was more than mushroom she smelled, for the Og family was actually enjoying that great delicacy – roast shoulder of mushroom with wild rabbit sauce. All the little Ogs were holding up their tiny plates, their big round eyes glowing in anticipation, while the father Og was carefully cutting large slices of mushroom and ladling out generous portions of sauce.

The smallest Og had already got his portion and was digging into it voraciously when the mother Og rapped his knuckles: Patsy couldn't be sure whether it was because he was eating with his fingers or because he had started before the rest were served. She sympathized with the small Og on both counts since these were two crimes of which she had on many occasions been guilty. The little Og looked abashed and began to sniff a bit and then, when no one was looking, stuck his small green finger into the sauce and licked it. A second small Og caught him at it and began to point and whisper and cry "Og!" whereupon *he* got his knuckles rapped.

By this time Patsy had craned her head so far through the opening that Snavely, who was still curled around her neck, dropped off, landed on the table, and tried to taste some of the rabbit sauce. One of the Ogs saw him, pointed and screamed and tumbled backwards off his chair. The other Ogs looked up in surprise, and as each one saw Snavely they scrambled from their seats squealing and stumbling over each other as they fled out a back entrance.

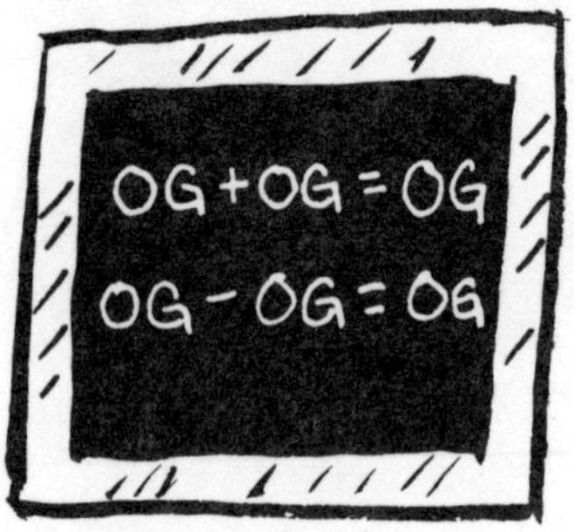
OG+OG=OG
OG-OG=OG

Only the smallest (and hungriest) of the Ogs stayed where he was. He began to gobble mushroom greedily, moving down the table to where the great platter sat and biting huge chunks off it, shoving the equally hungry Snavely to one side. When Patsy picked up Snavely the little Og paid no attention at all but kept on eating as if his life depended on it. It was the first time (and the last) that he'd ever been left alone with half a mushroom smothered in rabbit sauce.

As the little Og refused to make conversation Patsy squeezed back out the little door and sauntered across the street into a much larger building.

Here was a broad but empty room with rows of small seats and, at one end, a play blackboard, very similar to one which she herself had owned. On the blackboard was some writing in chalk:

$$\text{Og} + \text{Og} = \text{Og}$$
$$\text{Og} - \text{Og} = \text{Og}$$

And again:

$$\begin{array}{r}\text{Og}\\ \times\ \text{Og}\\ \hline \text{Og}\end{array} \qquad \begin{array}{r}\text{Og}\,/\,\text{Og}\\ \hline \text{Og}\end{array} \qquad \begin{array}{c}\text{Og}\\ \sqrt{\text{Og}}\end{array}$$

This, though Patsy of course didn't realize it, was the entire year's arithmetic course at the Og school. As it had been recess for the past five months, however, the school was unoccupied. It all looked very boring and so, absently swinging Snavely by the tail, Patsy walked back into the street and followed it down to a large open space. This appeared to be some sort of market, for there were stalls set up along the sides, with articles for sale.

The market place was in a state of confusion. Little green people, many of them grotesquely dressed, were rushing about in every direction as if in panic. The stall-keepers were shutting up their stalls and running about with their arms loaded with merchandise, much of it spilling on the ground. In their alarm, the little people clogged the street openings that led into the square, climbing over one another in their haste to leave. Some even rushed down and jumped into the river, which flowed past a few feet away.

At the cave, meanwhile, Penny and the others were facing a threatening crowd.

The green people had formed a semicircle at the outside of the cavern – a tight, silent mob dressed in dolls' clothes, Zorro capes, cowboy garb and other queer garments, slowly pressing in upon the children.

In the foreground, prone on the velvety turf, lay the body of Captain Hook.

"There's going to be trouble," Penny said, "now that we've shot one of them." A low murmur rippled through the crowd.

"I don't get it," said Pamela. "That gun won't shoot

anything. It hasn't even got caps in it. I don't think he's dead at all. See – he's breathing! Why, he's only pretending!"

"That's just it," Penny told her. "They're all pretending. They play Pretend all day long, and every day. But that doesn't change things one bit. They pretend things so much that they get to believe them. And if they *believe* he's dead and that we're to blame, then they'll get mean."

"Well, I think it's just too silly for words," said Pamela.

"It's not different really from us playing Dress-up and having a tea party at Polly's bachelor apartment," Penny told her. "It's sort of fun when we do it. And these poor little things really wouldn't have much fun otherwise. You've got to see it their way."

"I s'pose so," Pamela said, "but that isn't going to help us right now."

The crowd was muttering more and more loudly and Penny could hear phrases that seemed to come straight out of *True Cowboy Comics*.

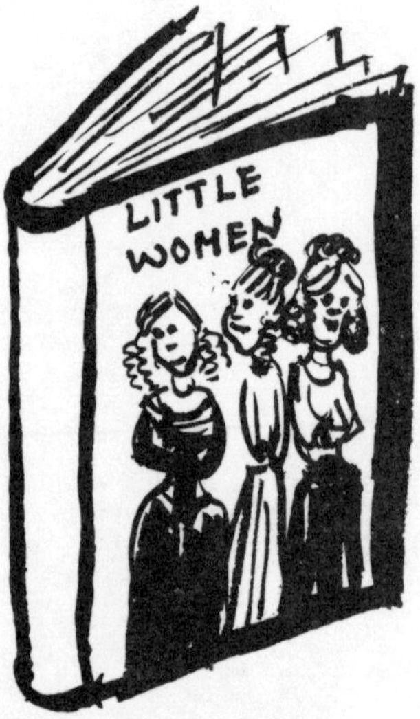
LITTLE
WOMEN

"They shot our boy!"

"Gunned him down in cold blood!"

"Why – he didn't have a chanst!"

"Let's git the varmints!"

"Run 'em out of town on a rail."

"String 'em to the nearest tree."

"Yeah – let's have ourselves a necktie party."

"Hangin's almost too good for these rustlers."

("If only they'd had a copy of *Little Women*," Penny thought, "how much nicer they'd sound.")

The crowd began to inch forward, growling and chattering.

"One more step and I'll fire!" cried Peter, entering into the spirit of the thing.

The crowd stopped.

"Let's rush him!"

"Careful, he's got a gun."

"He's a dead shot. Got that pore boy right through the heart."

"They got the Chief, too."

"Don't worry about me!" cried the Chief suddenly in a thin voice. "I am willing to die for my country. Rush these monsters and free our land from tyranny!"

("I wonder where he learned all that," Penny thought. "He *does* say it very well.")

"Git around behind them," somebody shouted.

"Cain't. They got their backs to the wall."

Penny now brandished her water pistol and stepped up beside Peter.

"Move back, all of you!" she shouted, "or I'll shoot!"

There was a flurry in the crowd and everybody edged back a step or so. Looking down the street, Penny could see that the mob was growing larger by the minute. How long, she wondered, could they hold them off?

"Yuh'd best give yerselves up!" the Chief said. "You can't shoot us all."

"They only got eight rounds left 'atween 'em," somebody else said. "He's already fired four."

That's right, Penny told herself. Peter had gone "Bang!" four times at Captain Hook. Fairly riddled him, she thought, forgetting it was all pretend.

"Come on, boys!" cried one of the green men in the front row. "Are we goin' to let them get away with it? Come on – all together!" And so speaking he rushed forward, the crowd surging behind him.

"Bang!" cried Peter, and the man who had spoken dropped to the ground, clutching at his chest.

"Bang!" Peter shouted again, and another green man clasped himself by the shoulder. "Winged me, drat his

hide," this man cried, and kept coming.

"Bang!" said Peter again but nothing happened.

"He's outa bullets!" cried a third man.

"Bang!" said Penny, pointing her water pistol at him, and he toppled over. But before she had a chance to fire a second time the mob was upon her dragging her down.

In a few seconds the three children were securely pinioned. The Chief, taking command at once, ordered the sheriff released along with the Pollywog, who was placed under guard with the others.

"A fine how d'you do, sheriff!" said the Chief sternly.

"I had to think of my wife and children," said the sheriff, his nose running slightly. He looked about fiercely as if to make up for his failures.

"Them varmints'll pay for this!" he hissed, staring at the captured children, and wiping his nose. The crowd edged forward as the sheriff produced a length of rope, which Penny recognized as a worn-out skipping rope.

"Let's get it over with!" he cried.

"String 'em up to the highest tree!" shouted a voice in the crowd.

"Silly!" Pamela whispered, "there aren't any trees."

"All the same," Penny told her, "I don't like it one bit. They really mean it, Pam."

"What'll we do?" Pamela whispered.

"Well," said Penny, dubiously, "there's always Patsy."

"Goodness knows where she's got to!" Pamela said. "If she's going to save us she'd better hurry."

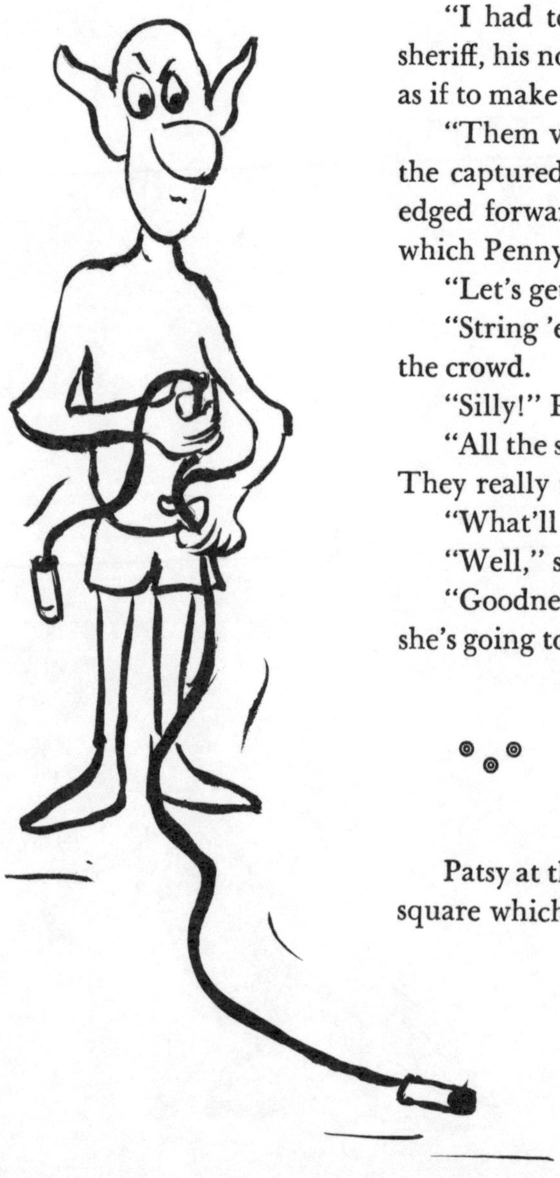

Patsy at this moment was standing in the middle of the square which was now quite empty.

"There's something real jalopy about this," she said to the animals. "People aren't usually this scared of me – even when I go cross-eyed. I don't think they were very scared of Penny. Else why didn't she come back to us?"

She sat down in the middle of the square to think about it. Yukon King and Earless Osdick sat down with her. Each of them believed that they had frightened off the people by being fierce, untamed dogs. They sat bolt upright, on either side of Patsy, trying to growl in a menacing fashion. Yukon King was pretending that he was Fang, Killer Wolf of the Klondike.

"Let's go down to the river and explore," Patsy said, scrambling to her feet. "Maybe we can scare more people," she added, wickedly.

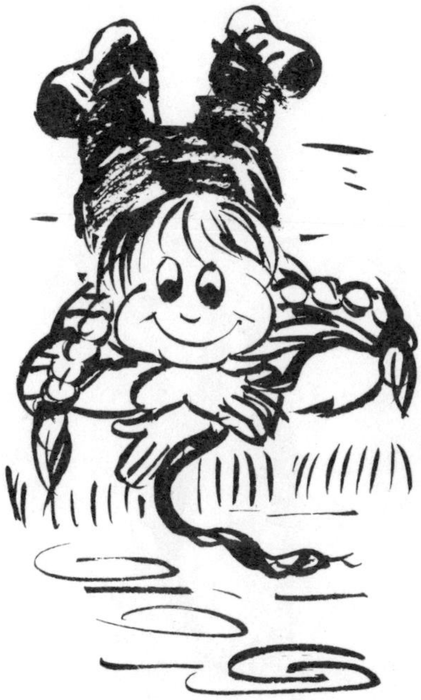

In her excitement she forgot about Penny and the others, and now, when they needed her so desperately, she skipped off toward the river, with the animals romping beside her and Snavely flopping about on her neck and shoulders.

The river was full of boats, moving up and down, many of them loaded with bright mushroom tops and others with dried mushrooms split into timbers. The boats had flat bottoms and there was a man in the stern of each with a long pole to push it against the stream or steady it in the current.

Patsy lay on her stomach on the edge of the bank and looked down, holding tight to Snavely who was doing his best to wriggle out of her grasp. A heavily loaded boat with two men in it was passing directly beneath her. One of the men looked up, saw her peering over the edge, screamed something and dived into the water. The other, without even looking, dived after him. Patsy squealed in delight at the spectacle.

She leaned farther over the bank to get a better view and – as she always did – fell in.

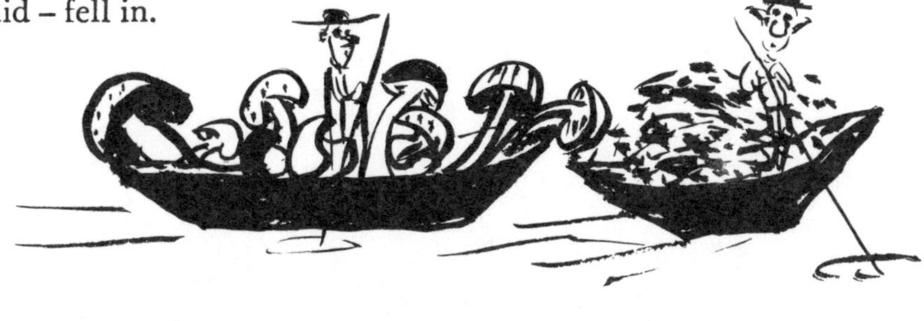

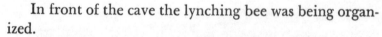

In front of the cave the lynching bee was being organized.

"Here, Red," cried one of the Chief's men. "Take this rope and string it over a good high branch."

Pamela began to giggle.

"He called him 'Red,'" she said, "and he's as green as grass."

"It's part of the game," Penny told her. "They change their names every week. They get them out of comic books."

"Well," said Pamela, still giggling, "he'll have a hard time finding a branch. There *aren't* any branches."

But Red put the rope over his arm and began to clamber up the side of the cliff. He hooked the rope over a ledge of rock just above the cave and let one end drop. A man below, wearing an old straw hat, seized it.

"Him first!" cried the Chief. "He's the one started the shooting."

He pointed straight at Peter who was pushed forward by several hands.

"Oh, Pamela, I really think they mean to go through with it," Penny said. "If only Patsy would get here!"

"They're scared of Patsy for some reason," Pamela told her. "At least the ones up on the hill were."

"I'll try to stall them for a few minutes," Penny said. She shouted at the ringleaders:

"Aren't you going to give him a trial?"

"Trial?" said the sheriff contemptuously. And he pointed at the fallen body of Captain Hook. "Did *he* have a trial?"

There was a murmur from the crowd.

"No, sir!" cried the sheriff. "None of yer Philadelphia lawyers' tricks in this burg. We mean to show you rustlers what true Western justice is!"

The crowd cheered as he placed the noose around Peter's neck.

◎ ◎
◎

Patsy wasn't in the least surprised by her sudden tumble. After all, it happened almost every day. She lost her bearings as usual and swam to the far shore before she realized that she was going the wrong way. She could see Yukon King and Earless Osdick on the other bank running up and down and trying to bark.

"Well, Snavely," Patsy said. "I guess we'd better go back by the bridge." But Snavely was no longer around her neck.

"Snavely, you bad snake!" Patsy said. "Where have you got to now?"

There was a motion out in the river and then she spotted him: a long slender wriggle of brown swimming strongly in the gentle current. But Patsy could see he was losing the battle with the river.

"Don't fight it, Snavely!" cried Patsy. "Drift down. I'll fish you out by the bridge."

And she headed down toward one of the piers of the little footbridge that spanned he river.

There was a great bumping and shoving and chattering going on above her on the bridge. Several green people toppled off the bridge and swam, fearfully, to shore. Others were looking out into the water and pointing and

crying "Og!" in trembling voices.

Patsy reached into a moored boat and pulled a long mushroom stick off the top of a pile. Then she waded out into the water, and hooked Snavely as he came by. As she did so she could hear, somewhere in the distance, the shouting of a great crowd.

As the noose went around Peter's neck the crowd gave a mighty, bloodthirsty cheer. Penny was desperately trying to remember something she'd read in *Lucy Lawless, Girl Rustler*.

"Just a moment!" she shouted. "You ought to give him a chance to make a farewell speech! It's done all the time," she added hastily.

And, indeed, in the Lucy Lawless incident that farewell speech had given Lucy just the time she needed to make her getaway.

"All right," said the sheriff, grudgingly. "Make your speech but keep it short."

"Make it *long!*" Penny whispered to Peter.

Peter stepped forward and made his speech.

"I don't want to play any more," he said. And his lower lip began to tremble.

13/The Forbidden Word

Above Patsy the bridge across the river began to give way as the crowd scrambled for the opposite shore. It shook and creaked and then it broke in two, crashing into the water. There were shouts and screams of panic as several stragglers fell into the river howling in terror.

"Oh, dear!" said Patsy, who felt that, in some vague way, she was responsible for what had happened.

The people in the water clawed their way up onto the opposite shore and Patsy was relieved to see that all of them seemed to be able to swim. Only at the last moment did she hear a thin little voice crying plaintively and see a small green head bobbing about in the water.

"Why, it's a little green baby!" Patsy said. She stuffed Snavely in her pocket, jumped into the river and swam across to the infant. The little thing was threshing about wildly but Patsy, who was very wiry, had no trouble dragging it to the bank. She held it up by one toe and shook it to try to get the water out, whereupon it commenced crying again. Somewhere in the distance she again heard the shouting of a crowd but here, on the river bank, there was no longer any sign of people.

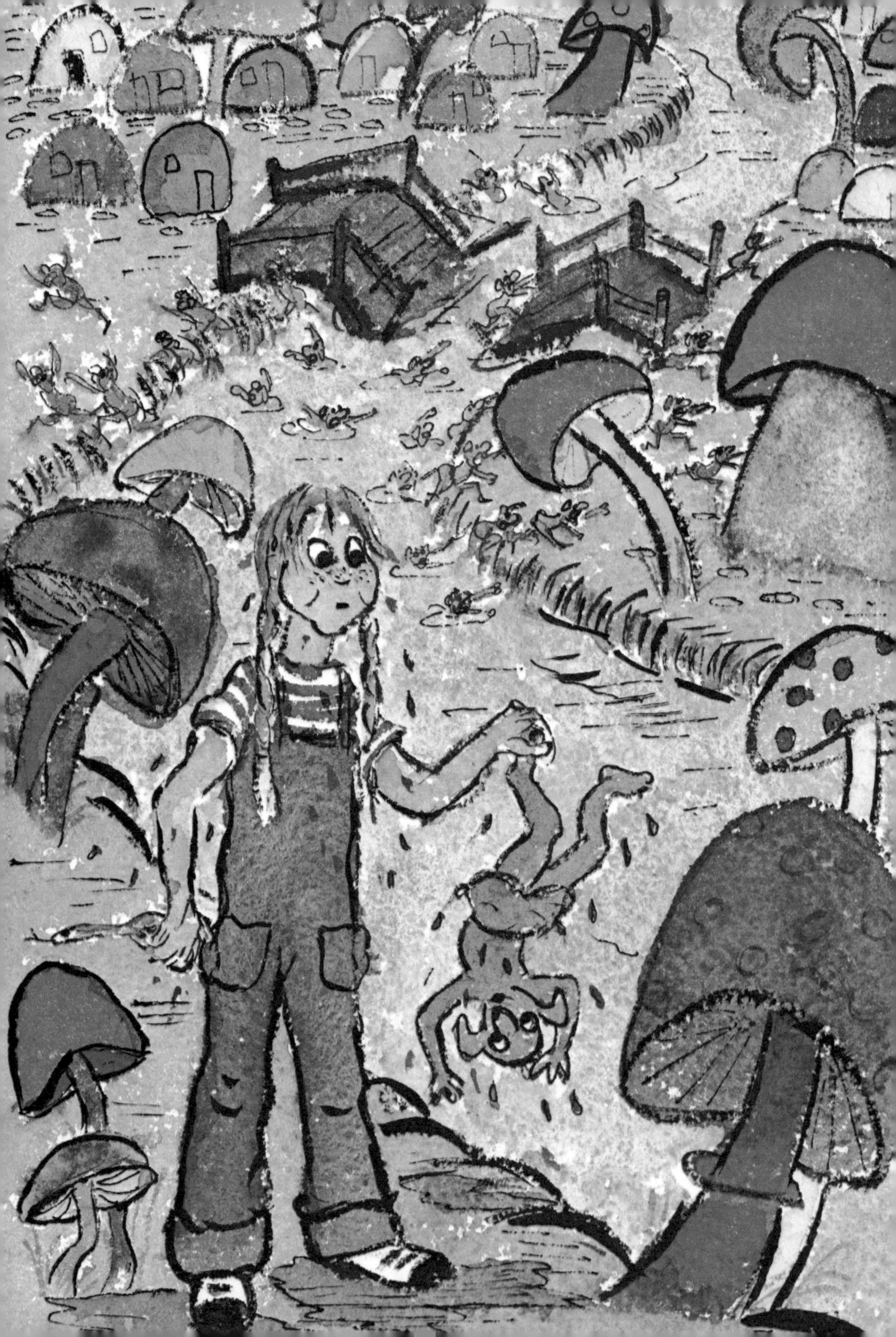

Penny was waving frantically at Peter.

"Keep talking, Pete!" she whispered at him but Peter had nothing more to say. His lower lip was still trembling. He looked as if he were about to cry.

"That's enough!" said the sheriff. "Haul away, boys!"

The men up above dug their feet in and the rope began to tighten.

"Oh, Pam!" cried Penny. "They really mean it!"

There was a scuffling off to one side.

"It's the littlest one!" somebody said. "He's got away."

"Grab him, quick!"

"It's Polly!" Pamela said. "He's escaped again."

The Pollywog was crawling off at a steady speed of six miles an hour but he wasn't fast enough. Two green men overtook him and, even though he bit one on the ankle, they brought him back.

"All right!" cried the sheriff again. "Haul on the rope!"

Peter stared wildly at his two sisters. He couldn't speak because the rope was too tight around his throat and his eyes were staring strangely as his breath was cut off.

His feet were just leaving the ground when there came a high-pitched scream and a green figure broke through the crowd chattering and shouting and panting heavily. The men with the rope dropped it and Peter fell forward onto his knees.

The new man, who was wearing a small boy's play suit, ran into the heart of the crowd waving his arms for silence. As he spoke, two more arrived, then several more, running down the street.

"GLOG!" cried the first man, in a voice of doom.

"Why," said Penny, "there *is* another word in their language!"

Captain Hook, who had been lying on his face all this time, jumped to his feet and Penny could see that he was several shades paler.

The others who had been shot also jumped up.

"They're not pretending any more," said Pamela.

The people crowded around their Chief, looking wildly about them, their eyes wide with terror.

Peter pulled the rope off his neck and ran over to join the others.

"Something really awful must have happened," Penny said.

She ran up to Captain Hook and took him by the arm. To her surprise she saw that he was trembling violently.

"What does *Glog* mean?"

"It is the forbidden word!" said Captain Hook, his teeth chattering. "It is so terrible that even I cannot speak it." And he began to wring his hands and jump up and down.

"Yes," said Penny, quite vexed at all the mystery. "But what does it *mean?*"

"It means," said Captain Hook, and he rolled his eyes in a horrible way, "that the Snake People have attacked us!"

More green people were arriving, all of them in terror. Penny ran up to the Chief and seized him by the shoulder. His mask had toppled off and his face, which turned out to be rather thin and wizened, seemed almost as pale as hers.

"They're attacking from all sides!" the Chief cried, to no one in particular. "They're coming down from the hills! They've infiltrated right to the public square! It's the end of all of us!" And he began to run about in a small circle, shouting "Doomed! Doomed! Doomed!" at the top of his voice.

"Oh, don't be such a silly," said Penny firmly. "Take hold of yourself. What would Wyatt Earp do?"

"You know these guns aren't real," said the Grand Exalted Keeper of the Holy Mushroom Patch, admitting it for the first time. "We've no weapons against the Snake People!"

And he threw himself on the ground, hiding his face in his hands as if trying to make himself invisible.

"Now *stop* that!" Penny cried, pulling him to his feet. She towered over him, being almost twice his height, and she felt like an angry parent scolding a foolish child.

"Surely you're not all going to just lie down and give up?" she said.

"What else can we do?" the Chief asked. "You don't know these . . . these . . . *Glogs*" (he whispered the terrible word in a small, husky voice), "they're worse than the Mad Monster!"

"How on earth would *you* know?" Penny retorted. "You've never even seen one. You've never *known* anybody who's seen one. It's probably all in your head, like Jesse James and Peter Pan and the other stories."

"*They've* seen them!" cried the Chief pointing to the groups of panic-stricken people arriving in frightened clusters. "They saw one swimming in the river, attacking the bridge. He tore down the bridge and ate one of the babies. They barely escaped his horrible, slavering jaws."

"It sounds awfully real," Pamela said, her eyes growing as big as saucers.

"Well, you can't believe one word these people say, I'll tell you that," Penny said. "They're just like a . . . like a bunch of little children," she said.

"Too bad Patsy isn't here," Peter said. "She *loves* snakes."

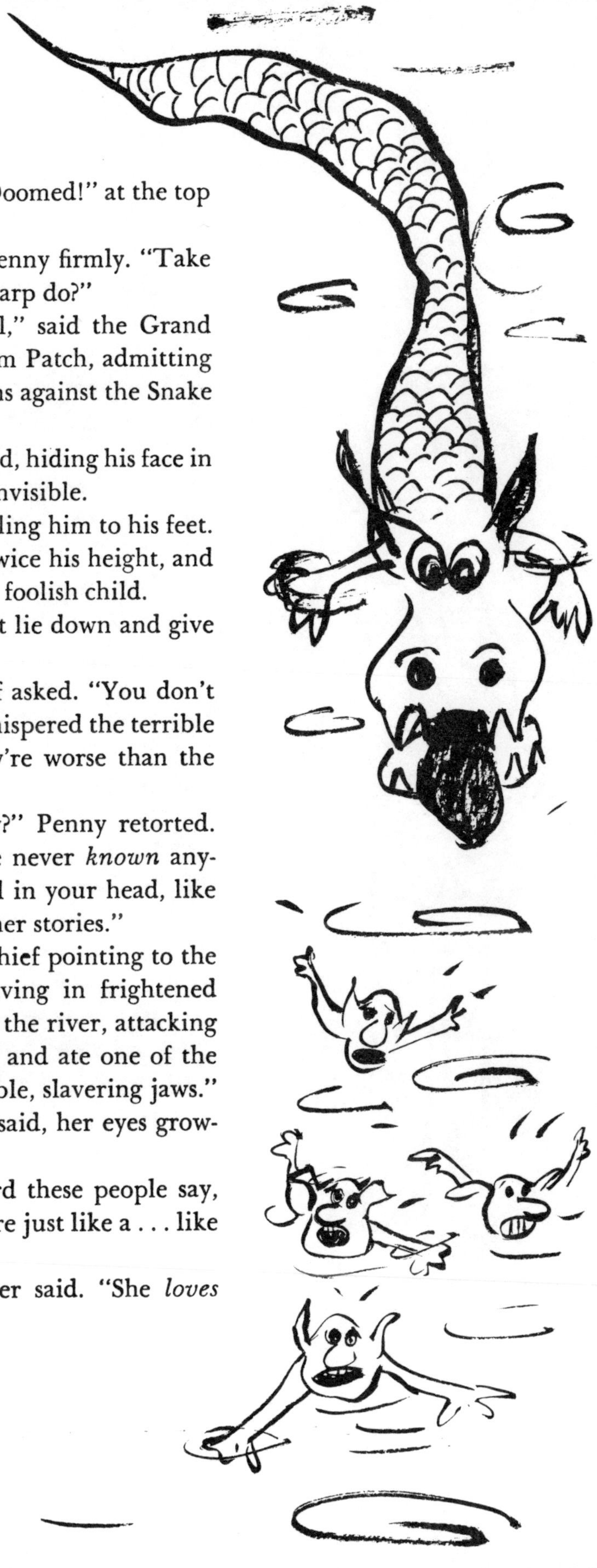

Penny stared at him, a light slowly dawning.

"Good gravy!" she said. "Pam – I bet it's little Snavely!"

"Her garter snake?"

"Of course."

"I bet it is too," said Pamela, nodding her head slowly in agreement and thinking it out carefully. "Now I remember – she had him out when she first scared those Greenies up above."

She started to giggle.

"They think Snavely's a whole army of Snake People!"

"Well," Penny said, "one thing about them – they've got good imaginations."

A thought struck her and she turned back to the shivering Chief.

"Look," she said. "We're not afraid of monsters. We'll save you from the Snake People."

"How?" said the Chief.

"We have a secret weapon," said Penny mysteriously.

"Yes, yes," said the Chief in distraction.

"Now," said Penny, firmly. "If we save you from the Glog we want you to make us a promise."

"Anything!" cried the Chief, "*if* you save us."

A whisper went through the crowd and the shouting and whimpering which had been going on subsided a little.

"We want safe-conduct home again and a promise from you that you won't use the tunnel under the Playhouse any more."

"It's a promise," said the Chief. "Cross my heart and hope to die," he added, hastily making the gesture.

At this all the Ogs crossed their hearts, solemnly.

"Oh, yes," said Penny, "and I almost forgot – I want Elizabeth Anne back. She's my doll."

"Anything!" cried the Chief. "Anything at all."

"And my cars!" cried Peter.

"Anything!" whimpered the Chief, "but please hurry. The Snake People have us surrounded."

"All right," said Penny. "All you people stay here. We'll drive the snakes back down the river."

"Come on," she said to Pamela and Peter. "Bring Polly."

"Now, don't worry," she said kindly, patting the little green man on the head. "You're all going to be all right."

The four children set out down the main street.

"I have a feeling we'll find Patsy by the river," Penny said. "She's probably fallen in – she always does."

"Look, Penny!" said Pamela suddenly. "There's Elizabeth Anne."

Penny plucked her doll from the unattended stall and hugged her to her bosom. "Oh, Elizabeth Anne," she said, "how glad I am to find you! Were you lonely for your mummy? Did they feed you properly down here? Never mind, darling, as soon as we get home we'll all sit down and have some tea together."

Pamela looked with her big thoughtful eyes at Penny hugging the doll to her breast.

"I guess everybody has to pretend at least *part* of the time," she thought to herself.

Peter had already run ahead and retrieved the cars that he had sold earlier that afternoon to the stallkeeper. He stuffed all of them into his pocket except his favourite tractor.

"B-r-r-r-r – !" he said to himself, running the tractor along the edge of the stall. "I'm in my tractor. Working on my farm."

"C'mon, Pete!" said Penny cheerfully. "We've got to find Patsy."

"And Snavely, too!" Pamela reminded her.

They ran down to the edge of the river, Penny in the lead, and sure enough there were Patsy and Yukon King

and Earless Osdick and a small green baby all playing on the bank. The baby was cooing and giggling at something it held in its tiny hand. That something was Snavely.

"Hi, Penny!" said Patsy. She looked just a little guilty, and she felt that she had probably done something bad. But Penny and the others seemed overjoyed to see her.

"He's lost his mummy," Patsy said, pointing at the baby. "Isn't he cute? Earless Osdick thinks he's another dog."

The Pollywog dropped out of Penny's clutches and crawled over to the baby. "Og!" he said, making conversation. The green baby poked a finger at Pollywog, and waved Snavely at him. "Og," said the baby, in reply.

"Penny," Pamela said. "Let's go. We could be up those steps and back home before they knew we still weren't here fighting the Snake People."

"Yes," said Peter. "Let's go. It's almost supper time – I'm hungry."

"No," said Penny, firmly. "We can't go. We made a promise and we've got to keep our part of the bargain."

"Besides," said Patsy, "we've got to find the baby's mummy."

"Come on," said Penny, "we're going back. Patsy, bring the baby and Snavely. I'll hold Polly."

"But what if they start that lynching talk all over again?" Pamela said.

"We'll just have to take that chance," Penny told her. "But I don't really think they will."

"If they do I'll just scare 'em!" said Patsy fiercely. "They're scared of me, you know, Penny!"

"You just think they are," said Penny. "It's Snavely they're really scared of. They think he's something that he isn't."

"Well," said Pamela, slowly. "That's nothing new for these people. Or us either, I guess."

She thought about that for a moment as they headed back toward the crowd at the cave.

"Maybe it's not so much what you are, as what you *think* you are," she said finally, trying to sort it all out. "I mean, if you *think* you're something, then it's almost as if you *were* something."

"It works the other way, too," said Penny. "Look at Snavely. He knows he's a garter snake. But these people didn't know that. As far as they were concerned he *was* a monster."

"Well, then, that made him a monster, I guess – if enough people thought it . . ."

"It did for the time being," said Penny. "But we're going to change that."

By this time they were back among the green people – all of them pressed in a dense green mass against the rock wall, their big eyes starting from their heads in terror.

Penny climbed up onto a big rock by the cavern door.

"Now," she said, "all of you, listen to me. The Snake People are gone. They won't come back."

A shudder of relief passed through the crowd.

"As far as that goes," Penny went on, "there never *were* any Snake People."

Everybody began talking at once.

"There was one little garter snake," cried Penny, and she reached down and plucked the green baby out of Patsy's arms.

"And here he is!" she cried. The baby waved Snavely back and forth.

"Snavely loves this," Patsy whispered to Peter. "It's a big moment for him. He thinks he's the Mad Monster!"

"This is the baby that was supposed to have been eaten by a monster," said Penny. "And this," holding up Snavely, "*this* is the terrible Glog!"

14/The Pollywog Learns a Secret

There was a chattering of surprise in the crowd. Several had backed off at the sight of Snavely but these now crept forward again.

A little green woman reached up for the baby. The baby clutched Snavely and the green woman took them both. The crowd gathered about her, all talking at once.

Penny looked about for the Chief.

"Remember your bargain," she said, climbing down from the boulder.

The Chief had retrieved his false nose and comic spectacles and was busily adjusting them. He actually looked much better with them on, Penny decided.

"My word, madam, has always been sacred," he said.

"I think we ought to leave Snavely with you," Penny told him. "I don't think we could get him away from that baby anyway. Okay, Patsy?"

"Okay!" said Patsy, cheerfully.

"I was thinking," the Chief said, "of creating a new post. Grand Exalted Keeper of the Sacred Snake – or some such title. How does that strike you?"

"It strikes me fine," said Penny, suppressing a smile.

"We could have some sort of grand uniform to go with the post," the Chief said and his eyes took on a far-away look. "I might even accept the duty myself," he said, "if the people insist."

"It's my guess," Penny told him, "that there are no Snake People down the river. And if there are – why, what an adventure it would be to seek them out! Don't you think so?"

"Well," said the Chief slowly, "there's something in what you say. It's been getting a bit dull around here lately and we *are* in need of a new game."

"But don't you see?" Penny told him. "This would be a real adventure – not a game at all. You wouldn't be pretending. You'd be really exploring. Just think – that river must go on and on for miles and miles and you've never been down it. Who knows, all sorts of strange people may live along it. What an experience for the first man to find them!"

"It mightn't be so dangerous at that," said Captain Hook who had been listening to the conversation. "After all, we're armed!" and he patted Peter's cap gun, which he had picked up. "I'm a dead shot!" he said to Peter. "I'm a killer."

"Well," Penny thought, "he might as well find out things for himself," and having planted a new and adventurous idea in the green heads of the excitable Ogs she said no more.

"It's time we went back," she said. "C'mon, all of you."

"Oh, Penny!" said Peter, forgetting his hunger. "Do we *have* to go?"

"Yes," said Penny, firmly.

"Gosh, Penny," said Patsy, "we were just starting to have fun."

"Come *on!*" said Penny. "It must be almost supper time." To tell the truth, she too felt reluctant to go. It had certainly been the most exciting game they had ever

OG -

played. And now that it was all over, the afternoon seemed to have passed so swiftly.

"I wish it wasn't over," Peter said. "I wish I was back in my disguise again."

"Come on, Pete," said Penny, more gently. "Mummy will be worried."

The five children and the two animals started off down the street toward the stairs in the cliff by the river. Captain Hook bounced along beside Peter, making imaginary passes with his cap pistol. The Pollywog, who was the only one who spoke the language, conversed cheerfully with anyone who would talk to him.

"What's he saying?" Patsy asked one of the green people, curiously.

"He says that he's a dog and his name is Rover," came the reply. "He is a very fine species of dog," the green man added, seriously.

"I'll have my personal boatman pole you back up the river," the Chief said, as the group reached the foot of the steps.

"Remember now," said Penny, "You mustn't use the tunnel under the Playhouse."

"I promised on my word of honour!" said the Chief, in a hurt voice. "I crossed my heart!"

"You can use the other tunnels, though," Penny said quickly. "And anything you find left around you can have. It will teach the little kids to pick up their stuff before nightfall." She had just about decided that she would leave her set of Lucy Lawless books out; she was growing a bit tired of them anyway.

They had reached the top of the stairs and the ledge of rock where Penny had first been taken prisoner.

"Well," said Penny, "I guess we'll say good bye," and she wondered why she was feeling so sad.

"This has been the most exciting day of my life!" Captain Hook blurted out and Penny saw that his eyes were misty.

She felt a funny feeling in her throat. Suddenly she wanted to do something nice for Captain Hook.

"Here," she said quickly. "Take Elizabeth Anne. She's my very best doll so take very, very good care of her."

She gave the doll a last hug and a kiss and then put her gently into Captain Hook's hands.

"The two of you can take turns playing with her," she explained to the Chief. "She has hair that really combs." And then, because she hated long good byes, she turned and walked swiftly into the tunnel where the little boats were moored.

"I'm sorry my boatman doesn't speak your language," the Chief said to Pamela. "But he was too lazy to learn. That is the way with young people nowadays."

The boatman stepped forward with a shy grin.

"Hi, Og," said Peter, recognizing him at once.

How different he looks now, Pamela thought to herself; not a bit fearsome or lizard-like, as we all thought when we first saw him.

The boatman was still clutching the battered toy sailboat and now he handed it to Peter.

"You can keep it," said Peter, not to be outdone by Penny's sacrifice.

But Og thrust the boat firmly into Peter's hands as he led the way into the tunnel.

"Good bye!" cried Captain Hook and the Chief in one voice.

And the children turned and waved good bye.

"Let's come back tomorrow!" cried Patsy.

"No," said Pamela slowly as they climbed into the boat. "That's one game we couldn't play again. It just

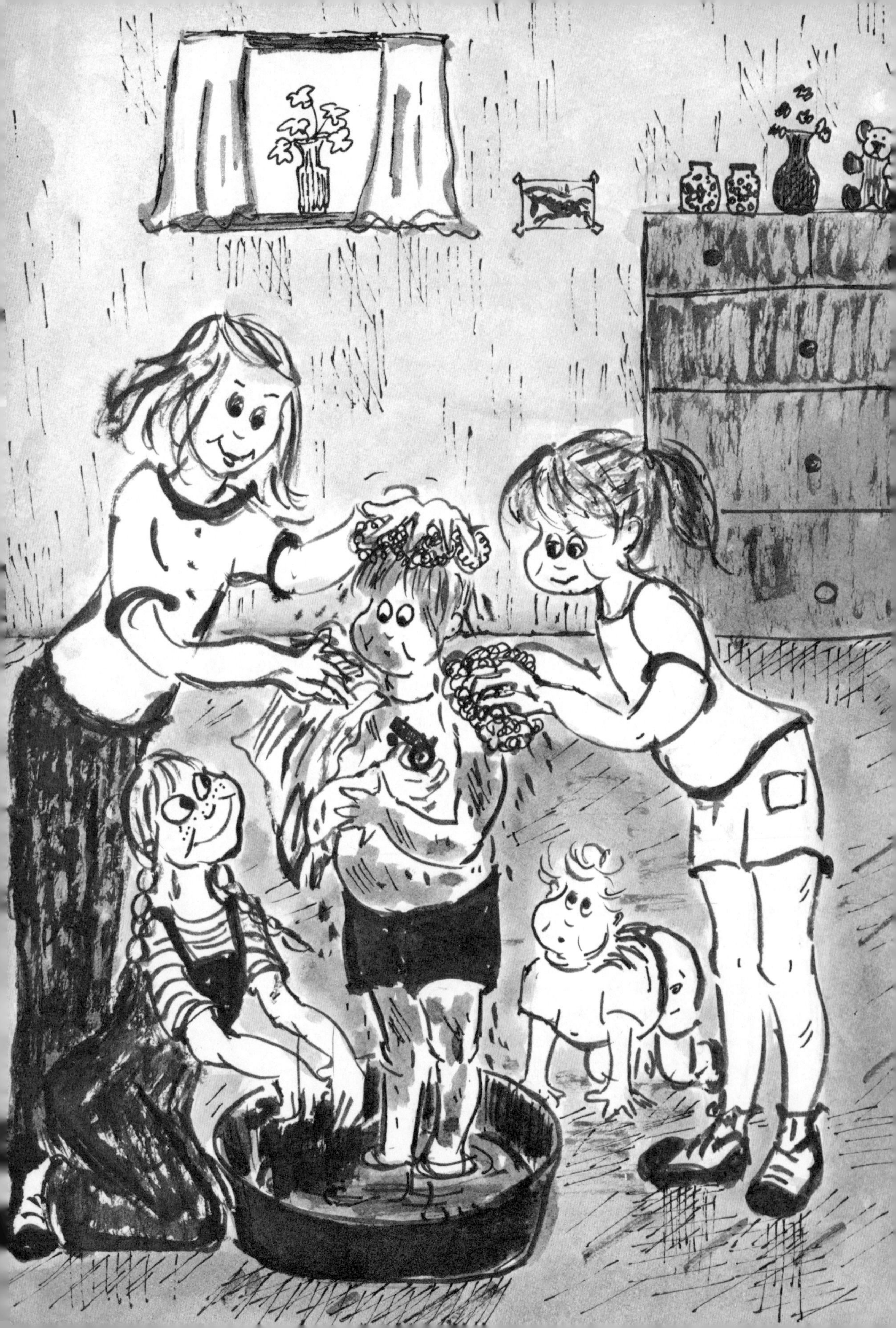

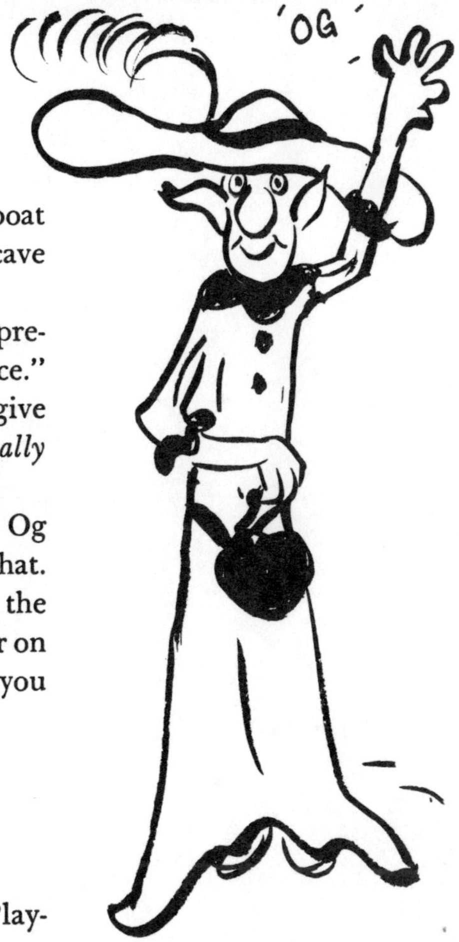
'OG'

wouldn't be the same."

"I see the Dress-Up clothes!" shouted Patsy as the boat emerged from the dark tunnel and into the glowing cave where they had first entered the water.

"Let's put them back on," said Pamela. "We can pretend we're society ladies climbing the stairs of the Palace."

"You can if you want," said Penny. "I'm going to give my dress to Og." (*I wonder,* she thought, *if I'll ever really play Dress-Up again?*)

"Oh, doesn't he look funny?" giggled Pamela as Og shoved off, wearing a faded evening dress and a floppy hat.

"Well," said Penny thoughtfully, "I don't suppose the dress looks much funnier on him than it did on me – or on Mummy years ago, for that matter. It all depends how you look at things."

"Bye, Og!" said Peter.

"Og!" cried Og from midstream.

"Bye!" the children cried.

"Og!" shouted the Pollywog.

And a few minutes later they were all back in the Playhouse again.

"Get a scrubbing brush and some soap and water," Pamela said to Patsy. "We've got to get the green off Peter."

"Oh, jalopy!" said Patsy. "I'd forgotten he was green. I guess I got used to it."

"Well, Mother won't be used to it," Pamela said crisply, and Patsy couldn't help thinking how very like Penny she was beginning to sound.

And so they scrubbed and scrubbed and scrubbed and most of the green came off Peter. He was sorry to see it go for in the world of the Ogs the colour had made him feel six feet tall.

"I can always pretend to be green," he told the others, "and then I'll be tall again." And he thought of that first bold moment when he had invaded the stalls in the little market in the strange world underground.

"Oh, won't Mummy be surprised when we tell them where we've been!" squealed Patsy, jumping up and down.

"There's no use telling," said Pamela. "Nobody'll believe us."

"That's right," said Penny. "Besides we promised them we wouldn't tell. Now remember, Patsy, it's a secret."

"Okay," said Patsy cheerfully.

"She always tells," said Peter, who was drying himself with one hand and running his tractor up the Playhouse wall with the other.

"She'd better not," said Penny warningly.

Down by the house a whistle sounded.

"Goodness!" said Pamela, "it must be supper. Come on!"

Peter jumped into his shorts and T-shirt and all five children scampered toward the house, the Pollywog crawling along almost as fast as the others.

Patsy dashed in first, shouting at the top of her voice.

"Oh, Mummy! We've had a real adventure! *Really!* We went down a tunnel and found a river and there were little green people all over the place and I scared them! Really and truly we did, Mummy! It was so jalopy!" And she sat down at the table panting with excitement.

"Really," said her mother, "sometimes I think that child has too much imagination! The stories she tells."

Patsy became very quiet – quieter than she had been all that day.

"It was just a game, Mother," she said. "A game we all made up together." And she looked across at Penny with a knowing kind of half-smile.

"Peter," said Mother, "what's that in your hair?"

"It's paint," said Pamela quickly. "We were painting

the Playhouse," she added, truthfully.

"Well, I don't see why he has to get himself covered with it. Patsy, your clothes look suspiciously damp. Did you fall in the river again?"

"Twice," said Pamela, truthfully again.

"Well, if it happens any more I'm going to have to dock your allowance, Patsy," her mother said severely. "How did Paul behave, Penny?"

"He was just wonderful," Penny said; and she meant it. She looked around for the Pollywog, remembering that she was supposed to put him in his high chair.

"Oh, my goodness gracious!" she said. *"Polly!"*

She pointed and everybody looked. In the living room the Pollywog had slowly risen to his feet and now as everybody watched he took seven steps forward, standing erect.

A look of pure astonishment crossed his face as he stood there, teetering. He looked down at his feet, and then he looked up at the family and then he looked over at Yukon King and Earless Osdick who were sleeping together, exhausted by the day's adventures.

For the first time in his life, the Pollywog realized that he was not, after all, a dog.

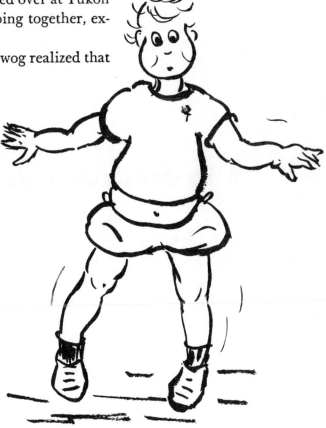

A Note About the Characters

All the human beings in this book are real.
The animals are real, too, though Yukon
King and Earless Osdick have gone to dog
and cat heaven. The Playhouse is very real,
too, but it has been moved deeper into the
forest and here, on a bright summer's day
you may easily find two little girls enjoying
tea, just as their brothers and sisters did
before them.